"Can't blame a man for appreciating what's in front of him, can you?"

Hank asked Jilly. "Besides, princess, I sure did like the way *you* appreciated me. Feel free to appreciate me all you want. I don't mind."

"How very generous of you." Jilly shook her head. "You know something, Hank Aaron Tyler? You're not a—a restful man to be around."

"Thanks." His grin widened. "I sure wouldn't want to be a *restful* man."

Jilly felt the blush creeping up her neck. "You're impossible."

"Not always…. Sometimes, sugar, I'm very…possible."

Dear Reader,

This month we have a wonderful lineup of love stories for you, guaranteed to warm your heart on these chilly autumn nights.

Favorite author Terry Essig starts us off with love and laughter in this month's FABULOUS FATHERS title, *Daddy on Board*. Lenore Pettit knew her son, Tim, needed a father figure—but why did the boy choose her boss, Paul McDaniels? And how did Tim ever persuade her to let Paul take them all on a cross-country "family" vacation?

Those rugged men of the West always have a way of winning our hearts, as Lindsay Longford shows us in *The Cowboy and the Princess*. Yet, when devilishly handsome heartbreaker Hank Tyler meets Gillian Elliot, she seems to be the *only* woman alive immune to his charms! Or, is this clever "princess" just holding out to be Hank's bride?

Anne Peters winds up her FIRST COMES MARRIAGE trilogy with *Along Comes Baby*. When Ben Kertin finds Marcie Hillier, pregnant and penniless, he gallantly offers marriage. But Marcie longs for more than Ben's compassion—she wants to win his love.

Jayne Addison brings us a fun-filled Western romance in *Wild West Wife*. And don't miss Donna Clayton's *Fortune's Bride*—a surprise inheritance brings one woman unexpected love. And, in Laura Anthony's *Second Chance Family*, reunited lovers are given a new chance at happiness.

Happy Reading!

Anne Canadeo

Senior Editor

Please address questions and book requests to:
Silhouette Reader Service
U.S.: 3010 Walden Ave., P.O. Box 1325, Buffalo, NY 14269
Canadian: P.O. Box 609, Fort Erie, Ont. L2A 5X3

THE COWBOY AND THE PRINCESS

Lindsay Longford

Silhouette
ROMANCE™
Published by Silhouette Books
America's Publisher of Contemporary Romance

To Wes's safety net: Norma Anderson, "Dr." Debbie Frey,
Colleen Lutter and Dr. Fee.
You made it possible to walk the high wire these last three
years and not fall. Thank you for a gift beyond price.

 SILHOUETTE BOOKS

ISBN 0-373-19115-4

THE COWBOY AND THE PRINCESS

Copyright © 1995 by Jimmie L. Morel

Printed in U.S.A.

Books by Lindsay Longford

Silhouette Romance

Jake's Child #696
Pete's Dragon #854
Annie and the Wise Men #977
The Cowboy, the Baby and
  the Runaway Bride #1073
The Cowboy and the Princess #1115

Silhouette Intimate Moments

Cade Boudreau's Revenge #390
Sullivan's Miracle #526

Silhouette Shadows

Lover in the Shadows #29
Dark Moon #53

LINDSAY LONGFORD,

like most writers, is a reader. She even reads tooth-paste labels in desperation! A former high school English teacher with an M.A. in literature, she began writing romances because she wanted to create stories that touched readers' emotions by transporting them to a world where good things happened to good people and happily-ever-after is possible with a little work.

Her first book, *Jake's Child*, was nominated for Best New Series Author, Best Silhouette Romance and received a Special Achievement Award for Best First Series Book from *Romantic Times*. It was also a finalist for the Romance Writers of America RITA Award for Best First Book. Her Silhouette Romance *Annie and the Wise Men* won the RITA for the best Traditional Romance of 1993.

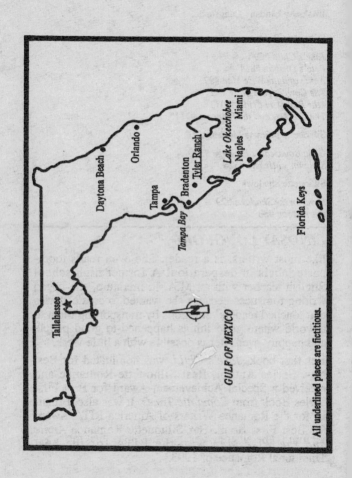

Tallahassee

GULF OF MEXICO

Daytona Beach

Orlando

Tampa

Tampa Bay

Bradenton

Tyler Ranch

Lake Okeechobee

Naples

Miami

Florida Keys

All undertined places are fictitious.

Chapter One

"You're drunk."

Opening his eyes, Hank Tyler stared into the deepest blue eyes he'd ever seen.

Trouble was, there were four of them.

Not that he felt like complaining, though. Lost in that soft blue, he thought that maybe everyone should come equipped with two sets of eyes.

Except they kept blurring in and out of focus, and when they did, that seductive blue dimmed.

He frowned and shut one eye.

Much better.

"You have the most incredible eyes, sugar," he said appreciatively, smiling delightedly at the vision who knelt beside him. The vision was peering into his face with a beguiling earnestness.

Lord help him, he'd landed in heaven and didn't even know it. Sun shining and blue eyes gazing into his from a face that would have landed ol' Adam himself in trouble.

"You're drunk," the woman repeated, her voice cool and a hair this side of censorious. She tilted her head and studied him.

"Is that a fact?"

She nodded slowly and a mass of dark brown hair swept forward, its slow movement entrancing him. "Very drunk."

"Angel-face, I hope to hell I am."

"You do?"

"Yep." He nodded agreeably as he opened both eyes again and watched that remarkable face blur and once more separate into two. He shut his left eye. "The better to see you, my dear," he said cheerfully.

She scowled at him, exasperation drawing the dark line of her eyebrows together as she sputtered into speech. "Why on *earth* would you want to drink yourself insensible—" She lifted a hand, dropped it. "I don't understand. Why—"

Watching her quick movements, he frowned. Something right peculiar wobbled on top of her thick hair, sparkled in the sunlight as she leaned back, but try as he might, he couldn't focus long enough to figure out what it was. Giving up, he answered her question. "I've been working my rear end off all afternoon to achieve this particular state of grace."

"A state of grace?" There it was again, that cool little tone of judgment and disapproval.

"Yeah, sugar, and one to which I've devoutly aspired ever since—" He stopped as laughter erupted from the vicinity of the house behind him. "Well, anyway, I'd be real disappointed to think all that work went for nothing." He crossed his arms over his chest and smiled contentedly as the breeze lifted a glossy strand of her hair. "Yep. Right where I want to be. Pie-eyed, skunk-drunk."

"You're lying on the grass."

Carefully, he turned his head and a clump of dark green tickled his nose. He sneezed. "Why, so I am."

She opened her closed fist and bits of damp blades fluttered to his cheek. "See? It's still wet from this morning's rain. Is this where you want to be?"

"Good a place as any." He tipped his chin toward the tree. "Shade, the sun above and thou, darlin'. Hell, if this isn't a state of grace, I don't know what would be."

Thick eyelashes rose, lowered, rose again, and her dusky blue eyes watched him thoughtfully as she added, "Lying on the wet ground. Good grief. And in your suit!"

"Lord in heaven, I better be in my Sunday-go-to-meeting suit. My mama'd skin me alive if I've gone and gotten nekkid as a jaybird." His chin met his chest as he raised his head to glance down his body. Scrutinizing his long length in the gray pinstripes, he frowned. There seemed to be two of him in his best suit.

Two of him. Two of her. Hell, worked for him. Seemed fair. Sighing with satisfaction, he let his head fall back. "Yep. That's my Sunday best, all right. Had me worried there, darlin'. Thought for a minute I'd gone and done something stupid."

"You don't think it's stupid to be, as you put it, 'skunk-drunk,' and lying flat on your back in the grass at a wedding?"

"Stupid?" Considering her comment, he watched the oak leaves overhead turn silver as the breeze rippled through them and moved across her shining brown hair, stroking it gently against her face.

"Yes," she said. "That's what I said. What I think. Aren't you embarrassed?" She straightened and two round nylon-smooth kneecaps flashed in front of his eyes.

Or were there four?

"Embarrassed?" He pondered the question. "Nope. Don't reckon I am, sugar. Takes too much energy and a lot more than this to embarrass me."

"That doesn't say a lot for your character. Or judgment."

"You're ab-so-lute-ly right." His tongue tangled itself in the words, but with an effort he got the syllables out in the right order.

"Aren't you going to regret this tomorrow?" Her face wrinkled with what might have been exasperation.

The color of the rainwashed grass around them, her narrow skirt tightened over her thighs as she shifted. Murmuring something that escaped him, she twisted, reaching behind her, and his gaze fell to her waist and hips, her legs.

Couldn't be heaven then, he considered muzzily, not with legs like that. Those legs were all but an engraved invitation to sin.

Nope, *definitely* not heaven, he decided as he watched the green fabric pull across the tops of her thighs as she leaned back. No panty line. Nothing but the smooth, curved shape of woman.

He turned his head for a better look. From any point of view, her legs were a miracle of nature. Yes, indeedy, he reflected, watching their sleek unfolding as she stood up. Enthralled by pleasure, he smiled. A miracle, for sure.

A bit of misty green lace at the hem of her skirt caught his attention, held it. Wherever he was, heaven, hell or someplace on earth, he was going to stay right where he was, listening to the flow of the woman's husky alto and watching her spectacular legs.

There were worse places a man could be than flat on his back in the sun with a vision in front of him.

He gave her a blissed-out smile. "Sugar, I wish to God I was sober enough to see if you're as downright delectable as I think you are. That's the only thing I regret."

He squinted, shut his eyes, rubbed them. Opened one eye again slowly, checking. Yep. A living, breathing sweetheart of a real woman. No hallucination.

"Do you often overindulge?" She folded her arms in front of her, long, small-palmed hands overlapping. On one slim finger an enormous ring glinted in the sunlight.

A shame.

But marriage seemed to be in the air.

He glanced up at the bright sky. "Is it a blue moon?"

She checked the sky automatically and then returned her gaze to him, her face pink with annoyance. "What do you mean?"

"That's how often I overindulge, darlin'. Once in a blue moon. Or thereabouts." He crossed his ankles as he watched the nervous agitation of her feet in their thin-soled green shoes. Had to be Italian leather, he thought foggily. They had that look of dollar bills pounded right into leather.

Blinking, he scrutinized her legs again as he thought he saw them split into four, one set chubby and short. He scowled. That was a first. Maybe he'd had more to drink than he'd realized.

"But—" She waved her arm toward the crowd of people on the screened-in porch and clustered around the tables set up on the lawn. "But today, of all days. It's your brother's wedding." The finger with the Rock of Gibraltar perched on it pointed to the porch. "You could ruin it."

Hank sat up slowly, carefully. The people in view multiplied, divided, blurred as a cloud overhead drifted past. "No, I couldn't. Wouldn't. Nothing could ruin this afternoon for ol' Thomas Jefferson. For sure *I* wouldn't." He glanced over to where T.J. and Callie stood in a patch of sunlight.

Callie was beside T.J., her arm tight around his waist, and she was looking up at him as though he'd hung the moon and stars for her. And ol' T.J. looked as if he wanted to swallow her up in one big gulp.

Resting his chin on his bent knees, Hank shut his eyes. "I'd never mess up this day for my brother. Not for anything in this world or the next."

"What about Callie Jo?"

Callie Jo. Now, *there* was the question of all time.

Wearily, he opened one eye and saw that the vision had stooped beside him again, facing him. The breeze drew a strand of her hair across his wrist. "You smell like heaven on earth, sugar," he said, ignoring her comment and breathing in the woodsy sweetness that drifted to him as he lifted the silky curl of hair. He didn't want to talk about Callie.

"Can't you answer?" Her mouth was pursed in such concern that he was sorely tempted to lean forward and kiss it.

He'd probably fall flat on his face if he did.

"Sorry, sugar," he said, frowning. Her mouth was so rosy and full, he couldn't seem to see anything else. He shook his head, trying to clear it, and the rosy softness became a dizzying blur. "Reckon I've gone and lost the thread of our conversation. What were you saying?"

"Callie Jo," she repeated patiently. "Aren't you concerned you might be ruining the day for her?" A ruffle of green moved back from her arm as she waved her hand again toward the couple, and the diamond on her finger flashed and sparkled. The shadowy tenderness of her underarm vanished as her hand fell once more to her lap. "And after they've been through so much." Her voice was wistful.

"Did Callie send you over to talk with me?"

"No. I saw you walk smack into the tree and bounce off it. You slid to the ground and didn't get up. I thought you were hurt. Until I—" Her hands fluttered, communicating what she wasn't saying. *Until she'd seen that he was drunk.* "Anyway, Callie didn't ask me to say anything to you. I don't think she even saw what happened." The woman glanced worriedly in the direction of the bride. "I hope not, anyway."

Rolling his head sideways and tucking his face inside the barricade of his arms, Hank stared across the expanse of the yard toward his sister-in-law.

She was nuzzling the neck of his six-month-old nephew, Charlie, T.J.'s son. They were laughing as the baby gurgled happily and pulled at her neckline with one dimpled hand. Charlie had spit up on the shoulder of Callie's creamy-white dress, and T.J. was sponging the stain where it spread to her breast, his fingers lingering a little as he gave her a look that Hank understood too well.

It was a look that promised all kinds of things.

It was a look that said *later*.

Well, T.J. would have his *later*. He'd waited long enough. He'd been through hell and back and had never quit loving her. He deserved Callie.

And Callie?

It seemed, in spite of everything, all she'd ever wanted was T.J. After all these years, they'd found each other again. A miracle of sorts.

Another burst of laughter came from the porch.

Hank looked away, glanced down at his clenched hands, forced them open. "Sorry, darlin', I keep drifting off, don't I?" He shot his best smile at her and raised an eyebrow, inviting her to join his self-mockery.

Her voice was gentle. "That happens."

He lifted his head too quickly, glaring at her as tree and blue sky and glorious eyes went tilt-a-whirl. "What do you mean?"

"When you're pie-eyed, skunk-drunk." The expression on her face was uncomfortably close to sympathetic. "That's all."

"I remember. You're worried I'm going to spoil the festivities." Deliberately, Hank leaned back on both elbows and tapped the polished toes of his shoes together as he spoke, drawing out the syllables and teasing her. "Real thoughtful of you, but sugar, I'm so damned festive I can't see straight."

"I noticed." At the corners of her mouth, a smile trembled, pulling up the edges of her bottom lip, then vanished.

Disturbed by the gentleness in her voice, he leaned back farther, turning to the side on one elbow, and patted the ground beside him invitingly. "Only one thing would make me more festive." His grin was so big and wide, his teeth hurt. "Why don't you join me? We could—" He paused and gave the grass one last pat as he held her gaze. "Be festive together? You and me? In the spirit of the occasion?"

"I don't think so." She shook her head. "That wouldn't be a good idea."

"Lots worse," he said, watching the way her hair shone in the sunlight. Like being alone tonight, he thought, working hard to keep his smile in place. No. He didn't want to be by himself tonight.

Even a bottle of bourbon wouldn't get him through this night.

He gave it one more try. "Be a shame to end the celebration early."

"Possibly," she said. "But no, no."

She'd understood the message underneath his words, and she shook her head again, vigorously, not looking at him.

The thing on top of her head wobbled. And after a second, Hank realized it wasn't the effect of the very excellent bourbon he'd been sipping all afternoon courtesy of his brother's hospitality. "Darlin', don't mean to be rude, but what in sam hill is wrong with your head?" He half sat up and reached out his hand.

"It's her crown," a childishly high voice informed him. "She's a princess."

Bewildered, Hank shook his head. Now he was hearing the vision in some kind of weird stereo.

"And I'm a princess, too. Can't you tell?" Frowning censoriously, much as the vision had earlier, a round-faced girl-child poked her head around the slim hip of the woman. "Princesses wear crowns."

"I see."

"*Everybody* knows that."

"I didn't."

"Now you know. That's why me and Mommy got our crowns today. We're princesses."

Pink skipped along the woman's high cheekbones, and her hand jerked to the top of her head and pulled free a silver cardboard crown from a local hamburger drive-through.

"Oh, heavens. Gracie!" She shrugged and gathered the little girl into her arms. "I forgot." She folded the cardboard piece into quarters, not looking at Hank as her fingers twisted and poked at the stiff crown.

Finally understanding how one set of the woman's legs had been short and chubby, and relieved to know that T.J.'s bourbon wasn't toxic, Hank contemplated the matching pairs of eyes, the thin oval of the woman's face, the childish roundness of the girl's. "Yours?" he inquired politely, nodding to Gracie.

Gracie's crown was precariously lopsided and her mother straightened it. "Mine," she said, and her attention was all for the little girl standing quietly in the circle of her arms. "Gracie was hungry after we left the church. I didn't know how long it would be until—" She halted, rushed into speech, chilliness vanishing in her haste. "We stopped. And then—" she was clearly embarrassed "—we were playing." She looked in every direction except at Hank. "Gracie likes to pretend. Make-believe. She wanted to play princess. Because of the wedding, you see."

Hank didn't see at all, but he liked the way the rosy color brushed the delicate contours of the woman's face.

Her ring captured his attention again.

Gracie's mom.

Everybody was married. Or getting married. Except him and his oldest brother, Buck. The Three Musketeers were down to two.

Her hand fluttered inches away from his face. It was a really big diamond with lots and lots of not-so-small ones around it.

"Nice ring. You're married," he said, and the regret that nibbled at the edge of his consciousness surprised him.

"Yes." She buried her face in her daughter's wispy po-
nytail. "No."

"I understand," Hank said, but he didn't.

Gracie reached up and curled her chubby arm around her
mother's neck and leaned into the curve of the woman's
breast. Even tucked into her mother's arms, Gracie seemed
sturdily independent, her small face studying him carefully as she apparently reserved judgment. A smear of
barbecue sauce decorated one side of Gracie's yellow dress,
and the hem dangled from a triangular tear along its edge.

"Was." Blue eyes tinged with confusion and sadness and
maybe, he thought, a touch of desperation, finally peeked
at him from behind the safety of Gracie's crown. "Was,"
she repeated. She stood up suddenly, all the lovely
smoothness of legs and hip rising in one flow.

The woman didn't have a clumsy bone in her body, Hank
decided, and abruptly changed his mind, reaching out a
hand to steady her as she turned, caught her heel in a tuft
of slick grass, stumbled, turned again and landed on the
grass beside him, one curved calf draped over his thigh, his
hand cupped around the slope of her fanny.

The fabric of her dress was smooth, silky. And underneath, supple warmth tempting him to linger. "Sorry," he
muttered, giving her an apologetic glance as he withdrew
his hand. He stared bemusedly at his palm where his skin
tingled, buzzed.

Bourbon had never done that to him before.

Shooting her a look, he registered the heat in her face.
Her skin looked as if it buzzed, too.

Eyes, mouth, *her.* Soft.

"Thanks for taking me up on my invitation, sugar," he
drawled to the vision, enjoying her frantic movements as
she tugged at her dress and tried to untangle herself from
him.

"Mommy? What are we doing?" In a flutter of petti-
coats and tanned legs, Gracie somersaulted onto her

mother's lap and settled there with a wiggle of skirt and shoulders.

"If I were any kind of a gentleman, I'd pretend I'm not enjoying my—" He stopped as Gracie's gaze lifted to his. Clearing his throat, he said, "But I could always pretend I'm the gentleman my mama tried to teach me to be. Might be hard, though," he added, casting one last, lingering glance at green lace and curved thigh as she scrambled away, Gracie clutched in her arms.

"You're a flirt," she scolded. Her face was bright pink, her expression flustered.

"Yes, ma'am, I am." Hank nodded. "Like my daddy before me." He gave her a devilish smile, tickled by the way scarlet heat flushed from her neck right up to her cheekbones.

The discarded crown lay between them and he nudged it with his hand. His fingers still tingled from that brief contact. "Lost something, princess?"

Collecting her composure, she plucked the shredded crown from the grass and stood up. The heels of her shoes sank into the damp, sandy soil. "Thank you." Her nod was so regal she could have been authentic aristocracy. "I can see you don't need any help. Forgive me for intruding—"

"Is it Mrs. Princess? Or Ms. Princess?" he interrupted as he pulled himself to a standing position in front of her, blocking her exit. He wasn't quite ready to say farewell to his vision. Standing over her, he was surprised to find the top of her head below his chin. From his position on the ground, she'd seemed model tall, but in fact she was shorter than he'd figured.

Even in those ridiculously appealing heels.

He'd liked the height.

He liked the reality, too, he decided as the breeze lifted her hair, and that sweet, fresh scent of forest and flowers drifted to him again, the fragrance like nothing store-bought, more the essence of *her*.

"Or do princesses have first names?" Brushing his hand down his slacks, he stuck out his hand.

Her right hand rested on Gracie's shoulder. Smoothing the wrinkles in the material of her daughter's dress, the woman hesitated, as if she wasn't sure she wanted to give him her name.

He wondered if she would leave him standing there with his hand out like some pantomime artist. "I'm T.J.'s younger brother, Hank," he encouraged. "The black sheep of the family."

"I know." She gave him her hand reluctantly, and as he enclosed it, her slender fingers slid against his when she tugged her hand free. "I'm Gillian Elliott. Jilly." She tilted her chin, cool and composed in spite of the flushed skin and the flecks of grass clinging to her skirt. "Gracie and I are going to be here at the ranch for a few days." The chin angled higher. "With you."

"Are you?" Hank swayed forward. Taking a deep, heady breath, he beamed happily at her. A really rotten day had taken a slight turn for the better.

Her hand gripped Gracie's shoulder. "Go along and play, doodlebug." She patted Gracie, sending her toward the group of children on the porch swing. "Didn't T.J. tell you?"

Hank didn't remember much of the day, much less what T.J. might or might not have told him, but he noticed the way strain tightened her husky voice, thinning it with anxiety, saw the tension in her slight shoulders and tried to think.

Trying to recall a vague memory, he frowned. "T.J. said something earlier today. I think." While he and T.J. were feeding the livestock, T.J. had said— What? Something Hank was supposed to know. Tugging at his hair, he tried to clear his fuzzy brain.

Jilly saw the confusion in Hank's green-blue eyes. This wasn't going to work. She'd been a fool to let Callie talk her into staying at the ranch, but it had made such sense at the time, and she hadn't been able to think of any other solutions.

But now she decided there must have been another way of handling the situation. Another way of coping. She wasn't without resources. She had skills she could call upon. She pinched the skirt of her dress, plucked at the neckline, pressed her fingers against her still-hot neck.

As Hank looked at her hands, she forced herself to make them remain still at her sides, giving the lie to her inner turmoil. Even three sheets to the wind, Hank Tyler saw more than he should.

And he was the kind of charmer who could make a woman vulnerable when she most needed strength.

Jilly smiled casually, slowing her speech as if the situation were of no more importance than the question of whether or not it was going to rain. "Anyway, it doesn't matter. What Callie said."

"Yeah?" He glanced over toward his brother and sister-in-law and back. "Something about Callie's friend," he said. "You, princess? You're Callie's friend?"

"Stay, Jilly. A week," Callie had said. "Possibly two, if Charlie's doing all right. Stay until we get back from our honeymoon. The ranch is big enough. Hank'll be taking care of the livestock. Give yourself some breathing space, Jilly," she'd coaxed. "It's fine with T.J. With me. And you won't even know Hank's around."

Now, staring up at Hank's eyes as awareness dawned in their sea-depths, Jilly didn't think Hank was a man any woman would soon forget. All that sunshiny devilment, but under it, a note of something darker that tugged at her.

Narrowing his eyes, he swept back his hair, the strands a blaze of brown and red-gold. "Yeah. It's coming back to me now." Stuffing his hands into the pockets of his slacks, he tipped forward.

Jilly stepped back. She couldn't help it. There was such a focused intensity in his laughing eyes, such cheerful roguery.

"You're the house sitter. Right?" He smiled, and the crinkles around his amused eyes became white lines in his tanned skin. "We're going to share board and—" He stopped, his smile becoming a teasing grin as one thick brown eyebrow arched.

Jilly's fingers clenched her silk skirt. She'd been right. This would never work. Men like him came equipped from birth to torment susceptible females. And their most potent weapon was the simple fact that they genuinely liked women, liked everything about them.

And teasing green eyes didn't help, either.

She took one more tiny step back, and he followed, his grin widening.

"I like to share, princess. My mama raised all us boys to share."

"I've changed my mind. I didn't think—" Still walking backward, she rattled on. "Callie suggested— It was only an idea. A possibility. I told her— I saw you bump into the tree—"

"What's the problem, princess?"

The back of her legs hit a bench and she sat down. "No problem."

Propping one foot on the bench beside her, Hank leaned over her. Loose-limbed, lanky and broad-shouldered, he blocked her view. She suspected he'd done it deliberately, for reasons of his own. Clasped loosely over the gray pin-stripes at his knee, his hands were at eye level.

Broad hands, long-fingered, callused.

They were competent hands. A workingman's hands.

She looked away. "No problem," she repeated. She knew she was talking too fast, and she couldn't catch her breath, but silence seemed dangerous around this man with the knowing, laughing eyes and the charm that transcended his hard-earned inebriated state of grace. "I changed my mind when I saw the ranch. That's all." She lifted one shoulder. "It's farther from town than I expected. I wouldn't be comfortable here," she lied, looking down at the ground where one of his polished shoes rested between the green toes of hers. She slid her feet under the bench and looked up to see him give her one more of those smart-alecky grins as he straightened.

Oh, he knew the effect that grin created, he did. In spite of the situation, annoyance stirred in her.

"Nothing personal, Mr. Tyler," she said, and let her gaze drift around the yard, over the fenced-in horses. "But I don't think I'm a cowgirl at heart." Tilting her head, she smiled up at him, making her voice a shade amused, a bit distant. "You know how it is."

"Don't reckon I do," he said, his voice as smooth as honey sliding over a hot biscuit. "Maybe you could explain it to me?" The glint in his eye challenged her.

"I'm sorry. Perhaps you wouldn't understand," she replied, giving him a tiny smile that was clearly not at all regretful. And not in the least apologetic.

"Yep. You're probably right. But why don't you try? Just talk real slow, princess. And keep the words down to one syllable, why don't you?"

Her tone of voice was so snooty that Jilly felt like slapping her own face. She was making herself sick to her stomach. She was truly burning her bridges behind her with a vengeance, and where she and Gracie would sleep tonight was going to be anybody's guess. The banks were closed. She couldn't use her ATM card. But there would be something she could figure out. Once she was away from Hank Tyler and his teasing that scrambled her brains.

"Go ahead, princess. And I promise to concentrate *real* hard." He shot her an encouraging grin. "I'm all ears."

"I know it's your home, where you grew up, I mean, but I'd be bored. You know, *bored,*" she concluded with a nod and a vague wave of her hand toward the horse corral and out to the pasture, as her voice trailed away into that dreaded silence.

"Think so?" His smile curled her toes as he continued, "Maybe you would be. Maybe not. 'Course, I'm biased.

This is my home, as you so kindly mentioned—'' he imitated her gesture and his eyes laughed at her ''—but life's made up of gambles, princess. And what's a little boredom in the grand scale of things?''

Off to their left, Callie Jo's laugh rang out, and his head snapped in the direction of that silvery sound. His attention stayed fixed on the scene as Callie and T.J. posed for pictures on the steps of the porch. The skirt of Callie's wedding dress fanned over T.J.'s arms as he swept her up, holding her close to him for one final snapshot, Callie's arm looped tightly around his neck. Upturned to T.J.'s face, Callie's was luminous.

Catching Hank's expression, Jilly felt as though the sun had dimmed. She shivered in the sudden chill. And wondered if Hank knew how often his eyes followed Callie's movements, how often he turned to the sound of her laugh, to the sound of her voice. He betrayed himself with each unconscious flicker of attention.

That yearning look in his eyes drained the laughter and teasing from his face, left it harsher, carved from stone. Bleak with a hunger that would never be satisfied, scoured with that hunger he thought he hid.

In a crowd, surrounded by friends and family, Hank Tyler was the loneliest man she'd ever seen.

Then, as if a button had been pushed, Jilly blinked, T.J. set Callie back on the porch step with a laugh and Hank turned away, reaching down with one hand to scoop up a pebble at his foot. He tossed it to Jilly, shooting her a wide grin as she caught it.

''Good hands, princess.''

Maybe she'd imagined his look of desolation. But on the hand still clasped around his knee, Jilly saw the white knuckles.

''Hank! Get your butt over here!'' T.J.'s deep voice startled Jilly. ''Time to kiss the bride before she pitches eighty dollars' worth of flowers out into this crowd of hooligans and we skedaddle out of here.''

Hank's hand flattened against his knee. "Can't quit ordering me around, big brother? Seems to me as if Callie's goin' to have her job cut out for her. You being such a dictator. Right, Calliope Josephine Tyler?" His voice was easy, casual, but still Jilly heard the way he hesitated over his sister-in-law's name.

Callie laughed up at T.J. and leaned against him in the same instant that he bent to her, their movements synchronizing, tuning unconsciously each to the other.

Swallowing the lump in her throat, Jilly saw the tenderness in Callie's face, in T.J.'s eyes as he tucked a strand of hair behind her ear.

It might have been a hastily assembled wedding, a catch-as-catch-can affair, but it was a *marriage*. Jilly's eyes stung as she watched them.

Caught in a ray of sunshine that burnished their figures with gold, the bride and groom were momentarily isolated, as if enclosed in a place where no one else could ever intrude.

A world complete.

Loneliness washed over Jilly, too, another kind of chill in the golden October afternoon as she heard the gates of paradise clang shut, leaving her, like Hank, outside, forever alone.

Chapter Two

Swallowing, Jilly stared down blindly at her daughter who was tugging impatiently at her. Behind her, she sensed Hank's movement as he shifted his gaze from Callie and T.J.

"This is Nickels," Gracie said, clutching a grubby, thin boy with one hand while pulling at Jilly's skirt with the other.

Blue-eyed and more reserved than Gracie's exuberant bossiness, he hung behind Gracie as she dragged him forward.

"Hello, Nicholas," Jilly said, trying to focus through a blur of colors. There was no reason she should be so affected by that moment between Callie and T.J. Too much pollen in the air even after the rain, she told herself. That was all.

"Hey there, squirt," Hank said. "How's life treating you these days?"

"Fine." Hanging back, Nicholas rubbed one stubby-toed cowboy boot on the back of his once-creased gray slacks.

His white shirttail drooped over his skinny little behind. Like her five-year-old daughter, he'd decorated his clothes with barbecue sauce.

"He's my friend and I will go visit him and ride in his boat. On the big lake. And fish. His Jake papa said it will be fine," she concluded importantly. "But I want him to stay here with us this week at the ranch so me and him—"

"He and I," Jilly corrected automatically.

"Yes," Gracie said, nodding eagerly, "so I and him will have a wedding and cake and ice cream and balloons. And stuff," she added, pushing Nicholas in front of her. "Like today. And I will wear a long dress like Callie Jo's, only purple. I planned already. Purple's pretty. I look very nice in purple. But, Nickels—" Gracie put both her hands on her nonexistent hips and addressed the six-year-old "—*you* will wear a tuxedo like my daddy's. And your cowboy boots. If you like," she appended generously.

"Maybe. Maybe not." Scuffing the grass with a boot toe, Nicholas looked desperately toward the side yard where a tall, dark-haired man and a small woman with the same brown hair as his own stood talking with T.J.'s parents. "Cowboy boots for sure."

"And be best friends forever." Gracie shoved her hair out of her face and took Nicholas by the hand, smiling sweetly first at him and then at Jilly. "But first we're going to have a very nice visit. Here. Right, Nickels?"

"Yeah." Then, rushing through the words as he tipped his head up toward Jilly, he said, "Jake said a visit was okay with him. Sometime soon maybe. But me and Gracie had to check with you first." He took off running, his legs pumping hard as he barreled into the arms of the woman who'd hurried up behind him.

"Hi," she said, nodding to Jilly. "I'm Sarah Jane Donnelly. And this imp is mine." A smile curved Sarah's mouth as she swung her son up into her slim, tanned arms and laid her cheek against his straight brown hair. With one hand, she tried to stuff his shirttail back into the waistband of his pants. Off-balance, she staggered. "Whoof, buster, you're getting heavy."

"I'm Gillian Elliott, Gracie's mother."

A dark presence moved up behind Sarah.

"C'mere, sport," said the wide-shouldered, black-haired man who'd followed close on her heels. Taking Nicholas from her, he lifted the boy easily onto his shoulders. Nicholas leaned one cheek against the man's heavy, thick hair, cupping his child-size hands under the beard-shadowed square chin of the man who was unquestionably his Jake papa.

This man was all undercurrents and darkness in comparison with the Tyler sunshiny charm. Onyx to their bright gold.

Jilly thought Nicholas's Jake papa was the most intimidating man she'd ever seen, and she couldn't halt the backward step that bumped her right into Hank's hard chest. His light touch on her waist steadied her as she flushed with embarrassment.

"Jake's harmless." Sarah Jane tossed her husband a carelessly teasing glance. "Really. He's a sheep in wolf's clothing." Her eyes sparkled as she hip-bumped him. Even though he didn't smile, Jake's peat-brown eyes lightened as he looked at his wife.

"Yeah? A sheep, huh?" he said, his voice rough and low as he circled her narrow waist with one big, wide-palmed hand that wound up resting on the curve of her hip. "Think so?"

Sarah Jane rolled her eyes at Jilly and anchored her hand in the back pocket of Jake's conservative dark slacks. "All talk." She gave him a smug smile.

"Not always," he said, his expression as bland as vanilla custard.

Sarah Jane's face went as red as her dress. Wrinkling her nose at Hank, she pinched Jake's waist in retaliation. "Hey there, Hank."

"Hey, yourself."

Hank's long fingers stirred, moved to rest casually against the nape of Jilly's neck, just above the silk-covered tab of her zipper.

The skim of his fingers sent a small shiver down her back. But she didn't move. She had the oddest sensation that he needed to touch her, that, like her, all the *coupledness* was jarring.

"Staying out of mischief, cowboy?" Sarah's mouth pursed demurely even as she sent him a look that was pure devilment.

"Sometimes. What about you, brat?"

"I never get into mischief," Sarah said virtuously under lowered eyelashes as Jake hovered over her.

Jilly thought she heard a muffled snort from somewhere in the region of Jake's large self.

Hank shifted and as he did, his index finger slipped just under the silk neckline of her dress, brushing the skin. Jilly held herself absolutely still, not believing the aching need that sliced through her so unexpectedly.

She didn't want the sizzling heat that came from nothing more than the slight pressure of Hank's finger against her skin.

She didn't welcome the need to lean back against him, the need for human touch. She hadn't realized how much she needed someone. How long it had been—

"Weddings are irresistible temptations, though, brat." Hank interrupted her thoughts, shaking his head woefully at Sarah.

"Shoot, you *never* resisted temptation, Hank Aaron Tyler. Why start now?" Sarah Jane's straight brown hair trembled in the sunlight as she shook her head chidingly. And as she did, her husband brushed his hand down the shining length that fell past her shoulders to her waist.

"You're right. No sense changing the habits of a lifetime. A woman after my own heart, after all." Hank bowed gallantly, the gold-brown of his hair flashing in Jilly's peripheral vision as he straightened. But his hand never left

the curve of her shoulder and neck even as he continued
talking to Sarah. "And here all along I thought you were
nothing but a pest."

"Beast," Sarah said cheerfully.

"Brat," he responded, equally cheerful.

Jake's expression was wry as he shook his head, saying
only, "Children," in such a doleful voice that Jilly decided he was a man with his own sense of the ridiculous.

"I know. I'm a scoundrel," Hank said, a teasing skepticism riffling the surface of his words. "Should be shot for
the mangy dog I am. But my mama would skin you alive if
you did. She loves her baby boy." His hand was warm
against Jilly's skin, and she burned from head to toe, that
unexpected, teasing warmth suddenly making her want to
cry out.

Dropping her purse deliberately, she stooped to pick it
up, breaking that humming contact.

And couldn't understand why she was still aware of the
tall, lean man at her back.

"Anyway, Gillian—"

"Jilly, please." She felt the brush of Hank's suit sleeve
along her bare arm as he moved. Her skin tightened, and
the hairs on her arm rose, stirred by that slight touch.

"Okay, then, Jilly." Sarah curled one arm inside her
husband's, continuing, "Nicholas did invite Gracie to visit
with us at the lake sometime. And it's all right with us, if
you're agreeable to the plan." She patted her son's foot
dangling near her shoulder. "I'm a cousin of these rascally
Tyler boys." She tipped her chin toward Hank and T.J. and
then toward a man with dark red hair. "I'd explain how,
but it's one of those convoluted southern genealogies, and
I'm sure you aren't—*Jake,*" she scolded. "Stop that." She
plucked at the hand edging up her rib cage.

The way Sarah Jane's mouth softened, though, told Jilly
that the admonition was only halfhearted.

"Whatever you say, sweetheart." His rough, deep voice was meek, and he never cracked a smile, but there was nothing meek about the heat in his eyes.

Jake was obviously a man who needed to be within touching distance of his wife. In spite of her square hands and capable manner, Sarah had a poignant fragility about her. The way Jake sheltered her with the angle of his wedge-shaped shoulders and muscular body spoke of emotions that ran deep and powerful.

Jilly shut her eyes.

Hank was right. Everybody was married.

She should never have come to Callie's wedding.

How could she have known that she would be affected like this, that she would feel so, so *empty* in a crowd of people?

An old loneliness was curling low down and mean inside her, creating a cold that heat couldn't erase, a loneliness that had spread, sending its icy tendrils deep into her soul over the last seven months.

Opening her eyes, she caught the quick exchange of glances between Sarah and Jake, the stroke of his finger against her cheek, the gleeful thump of Nicholas's fist against his father's head.

People were wrong. *Wrong.*

Time didn't heal, it only shoved the aching need deeper.

Even with Hank's light touch against her neck, she wanted to weep for the sense of absolute aloneness that filled her.

Sarah clamped one small hand on top of Jake's adventuring one. She spoke slowly, apparently searching for words. "Jilly, we're kind of isolated down at Okeechobee. Nicholas hasn't had a chance to form many friendships with kids his age, so, maybe selfishly, Jake and I liked the idea of letting the kids get together for a visit. We thought Nicholas would enjoy being here at the ranch, and I need to let Nicholas out of my sight for his good and for mine."

Her bright eyes clouded over. "Jake tells me I can be a tad overprotective with Nicholas."

"I know what you mean," Jilly murmured. "These days it's difficult not to be." Still, Sarah Jane seemed like the last person to be a worrywart.

"Gracie is a sweetheart, and the two of them have been glued to each other today." She looked at Jilly with an unstated apology, and that hint of vulnerability Jilly had wondered at earlier vibrated in her voice as she said, "Anyway, it seemed like a good plan. But don't let the kids and us pressure you into a sleepover for them if you're not comfortable with it."

"We'll see," Jilly told her, wanting nothing more at the moment than to escape all the happy couples. "Perhaps. I'm not entirely sure what our plans are."

"*Mommy,*" Gracie complained. "No p'rhaps. That *always* means no," she explained, looking mournfully at Nicholas.

"Not now, Gracie. Please." Jilly caught her daughter's hand in hers. She knew the signs. She'd bumped up against her daughter's persistence since Gracie had first been placed into her arms, and lately Gracie had become even more insistent once she set her mind on some course of action. "We'll discuss it later."

"*Now.*" Gracie's bottom lip stuck out mutinously.

Ordinarily an even-tempered child in spite of her insistence on knowing all the whys and wherefores and howcomes, she'd had too much play and cake and too little sleep in the last three days. Easier to pass off Gracie's behavior as the result of sugar and fatigue, Jilly decided. Excess sugar and fatigue could be fixed. Other things couldn't be.

"Mommy, discuss it *now,* please, *please!*" Distress and temper pitched the childish voice higher.

As Sarah smiled in sympathy, Jilly wanted to groan, but she said only, "Gracie, that's enough. This isn't the appropriate time. We'll talk later. I promise."

"Don't want to leave Nickels." Her independent, stubborn child dug her heels into the grass and sand of the yard. Looking up, Gracie gave her the most pitiful glance, tears welling up in huge drops.

Oh, her daughter knew her buttons, knew how hard it was for Jilly to deny her anything these days. Too much had been stolen from her young life.

Looking at the small, trembling mouth, the eyes filling with bottomless tears, seeing her own confusion and grief reflected to her from her daughter's face, Jilly was tempted to give in.

Oh, she was tempted.

Jilly sighed and put Gracie in front of her, turning to the three adults. "Excuse us, please. Gracie and I need a moment alone."

Folding his arms over his chest, Hank held her gaze for a moment, his face serious before one corner of his mouth curled into a small grin. "Sure thing, princess," he said, his voice light, good-humored.

Teasing.

Looking back at him over her shoulder, Jilly saw his grin, noted the I-don't-give-a-damn raffishness of his stance, the rumpled sweep of his hair turning red-gold as sunlight stroked it.

And she saw, too, that his grin never reached his green-blue eyes.

His very sober eyes.

There was an expression in their somber depths as he stared after her that Jilly couldn't decipher. Her step faltered even as she turned away from him and gave her attention to her tired, cranky daughter. "Come on, snickerdoodle. Let's go sit down on the porch swing and talk for a second."

Behind her, she heard Hank's slow drawl, Sarah's chuckle.

With every step, Jilly felt as if he were calling her back. She felt as if he'd reached out and wrapped his hand around her arm, staying her steps.

And with every step away from him, she sensed his gaze along the line of her back, her neck. Her legs. She was so aware of him that her steps shortened, her breathing sped up.

And she didn't like that sensation one little bit.

No, she thought, brushing back Gracie's hair. She *liked* it way too much.

This was no good.

Hank Tyler confused her.

"Princess?" Sarah Jane tapped Hank on the arm.

"Her daughter calls her that," he replied absently, watching the elegant sway of Gillian Elliott's hips under the shimmering green fabric of her dress. "A nickname."

"She looks familiar to me. Should I know who she is?" Sarah pivoted to look after Jilly as she opened the screen door to the porch and waited for Gracie to hop up the two steps.

"Yeah," Jake said, frowning. "Lawrence Elliott. Palm Beach or Naples, Florida. Rich. New money."

The porch door slammed.

Hank rocked back and forth on his heels, waiting. Jake might or might not tell what he knew. If he didn't want to, nobody would be able to drag it out of him.

Except maybe Sarah.

"Don't be so stingy with information, Jake. I know you and that inscrutable blank look you get every now and then. You don't like Lawrence Elliott and his new money, do you?"

"Didn't," Jake said succinctly. "He's dead. An accident, according to the papers." And that was all he would say, no matter how Sarah coaxed.

The Donnellys wandered off to join the crowd that had meandered to the front of the house where they were waiting for Callie to throw her bouquet. Passing a big white wicker basket, Sarah and Jake scooped up a handful of rose and gardenia petals. Reaching up to Nicholas, Jake dribbled most of his into the boy's small hand. "It's a game. When Callie and T.J. go to the car, you pitch these at them, okay, sport?" Jake sprinkled the last of his petals all over Sarah Jane's smooth brown hair. "Like this, see?"

"Yeah." Nicholas let fly with a fistful of pink-and-white petals, covering Sarah's dress.

The sound of their voices vanished as they disappeared around the corner of the ranch house.

The breeze lifted the rose petals on the ground, swirling them up, turning them into streamers of color.

The pink was the color of Jilly's skin when she blushed.

Hank looked around at the suddenly empty yard. In the quiet, he heard the squeak of the porch swing, the husky murmur of Jilly's voice as she talked to Gracie.

Funny how alien he felt now in this place where he'd grown up, spent nineteen years of his life.

He could still remember dusty summers with grass and straw sticking to his bare skin, itching, and him shrieking like a wild man. Then he would dive right back into the straw with T.J. and sometimes Buck piling on, wrestling until the three of them were red-faced and sweaty, whooping with laughter.

He'd always expected to be a rancher like T.J. Like their dad.

Once upon a time, well, back when he was a kid, God, how he'd loved this place.

But then, except for holidays, he'd begun staying away from home. He'd traded his cowboy boots and dreams for airplanes and adventure, swapping the rootedness of this place and its dusty green ground for blue skies and freedom.

He knew to the day when he'd made that bargain with himself. Thinking of the twists and turns that time and fate had handed him, he sighed. Hindsight. Always twenty-

twenty. But he still believed he'd made the right decision; it had been the only one possible at the time.

Hands in his pockets, Hank listened to the rhythmic squeaking of the swing.

It was going to be a long, long week.

Unless . . .

He told himself it was an impulse only.

He told himself he didn't care one way or the other.

But he found himself moseying over toward the screen door of the porch. Found himself opening it slowly. Saw his too-tight grip on the door handle and made himself relax.

And as he looked at Gillian curled in the swing with her daughter in her lap, he discovered that he didn't intend to let her back out of her agreement with Callie and T.J. to stay at the ranch for a week or two.

Nope. Whatever it took, he would see to it that Gillian Elliott fulfilled her commitment. Righteousness swelled inside him. He would sweet-talk her all around the barn and back if that's what it took.

An agreement was an agreement, he thought, congratulating himself. Making sure Gillian Elliott kept her promise was the least he could do for his brother.

He told himself he owed it to Callie and T.J.

But even filled with noble purpose, he knew he lied.

He wanted her to stay for himself. Because he didn't think he could stand the solitude of the ranch for a week with the faint scent of Callie lingering in its rooms.

He wanted Jilly to stay because of the way she moved, the curve of her hip swooping into those wonderful legs. Wanted the scent of *her* in the house.

And maybe, a little, he wanted Jilly to stay because of that quickly hidden desperation he'd glimpsed in her eyes.

"Hey, princess." He sank onto a wicker chaise longue and leaned back. "Thought I'd join you and Gracie." He slanted his head toward her, let his gaze drift over the rounded chin with its hint of stubbornness that Gracie had inherited. Crossing his arms behind him, he pillowed his head and watched the ceiling fan turn lazily above. A cobweb stirred at the edge of a blade. "Unless this is a girls-only party?"

Jilly's glance fell to her sleeping daughter, lifted to him. "No, I suppose not," she said, and her reluctance was clear in the stiff line of her shoulders, in the way she started to reach for the discarded shoes with the Italian script inside the arches.

"Good."

Callie liked expensive Italian shoes, too. She hadn't always been able to afford them, though. The princess looked as though she'd never worn anything else. Her shoeless feet struck him as shockingly naked.

One nylon-clad foot brushed the wooden floor of the porch, a shushing, quiet sound. It was a lovely foot, he observed, elegantly narrow and high-arched, the toes tapering evenly to the littlest piggy-toe. He almost reached out to tug at that small toe.

The swing moved, squeaked.

From the front of the house, he heard someone laugh, a sharp bark of sound, and his heart turned over. T.J. had earned the right to laugh, to enjoy every part of this day.

Hank sighed, let the silence build, knowing that silence would force Jilly into speech. That is, he thought, startled by a flash of insight as she didn't say anything, it would if she were like almost every other human being on the planet.

Sitting a bit straighter, he studied Jilly's smooth oval face as she rubbed her chin against her daughter's hair, crooning some unrecognizable song.

As effectively as if he'd left the porch, she'd shut him out with her wordless, made-up song.

And anyway, he thought, annoyed, the woman couldn't even carry a tune in a bucket. While Gracie's eyes drifted shut, he listened to Jilly's scratchy rendition of two calico cats hitchhiking to Kentucky.

The longer he listened, the more he discovered that there was something oddly soothing about her off-key singing.

"Nice tune," he said when the silence stretched between them once more.

"Hmm. Really?" She glanced at him, her eyelashes shadowing her eyes.

Hank was almost certain that the slight curve of her mouth came from satisfaction. He knew the quick glint in the blue eyes did.

"Did Cletis and Clem make it to Kentucky?" he asked.

"Perhaps."

"I see." He yawned. "According to Gracie, though, p'rhaps means they didn't."

"The ending changes. I never know what will happen. But I like singing to her." She brushed Gracie's hair back from her forehead. "And Gracie likes my singing."

"Does she?"

"Of course." Jilly spoke with supreme confidence, a mother secure in the knowledge that she was giving her child a priceless gift.

Hank tried to control the grin spreading over his face. The princess had no clue she was stone-cold tone-deaf.

Apparently, nobody had ever told her.

And watching the way she crooned to Gracie, the way Jilly's mouth softened and curved over the syllables of her song, the way her mink-brown hair slid against her cheek, Hank decided he wouldn't be the one to tell her.

Everybody needed illusions.

Relaxed in sleep, Gracie coiled into Jilly.

Hank let the quiet and Jilly's singsong murmur keeping time with the creaks of the swing seep into him, ease the tight band around his heart.

Some gifts were priceless.

Besides, a guy could get used to this.

His own eyelids drooping, Hank struggled against the need for sleep.

"Princess?" he said through a jaw-popping yawn as he stretched his arms toward the ceiling fan.

"Hmm?" The swing slowed.

"About this house-sitting thing..."

"Oh, that." She wouldn't look at him, but her tone didn't encourage him to continue.

"Yes, *that.*" He wanted to see her eyes, see what she was hiding. "Well, princess, I promise I won't have my wicked way with you if you stay at the ranch while Callie and T.J. are on—" He cleared his suddenly dry throat and wished he had another glass of bourbon. Water. Anything. "While they're gone," he finished.

"Oh? I'd be safe because *you're* going to restrain your— your *urges?*" Her voice was a little too innocent for comfort. "I'd have nothing to say about it? It would be entirely your decision?"

"Nah. Just thought I'd let you know I didn't have any designs on your winsome self, princess, that's all. And an exceedingly winsome self it is, too." He twitched an eyebrow at her. Leered. Tried to make her smile.

"Really?"

Deciding he didn't like the sound of those two exquisitely extended syllables, Hank veered in another direction. "Me being such a disreputable rascal, and all, I thought I might have scared you off."

"Excuse me?" Annoyance curled her cool voice. "You thought you might have *scared me off?*"

"Yep." Watching the angry red blotch her neck, he gave her his cheekiest grin. So the princess didn't like the implication that she'd been frightened off.

"Quite frankly, Mr. Tyler, you don't frighten me in the slightest. Not in any way. But perhaps—" she looked him over with a lady-of-the-manor tip of her chin that almost made him laugh out loud "—you're afraid I might have designs on *your* winsome self?"

"Feel free, princess," he offered. He couldn't quite resist the urge to keep needling her. He liked the way her eyes sparkled dangerously with anger, the way she seemed to come alive as if a switch had been turned on inside her, sending a current zipping through her, melting all her cool elegance and lovely reserve. "Anytime you're in the mood. Be my guest." He flung his arms wide.

Her look dismissed him. "I don't think I'd ever be in that kind of mood." But her gaze slipped away too fast. "And, no, you're not the least bit terrifying. Annoying, though." Her chin tilted higher, exposing the long, lovely line of her throat.

"Well, princess, what else was I supposed to think? You changed your mind so fast about staying at the ranch, I figured I'd plumb terrified you into thinking you wouldn't be safe with me here, too. Me being one of those nasty male creatures at the mercy of all that testosterone and stuff." Lying on the chaise longue, he yawned again, showing her exactly how harmless he was.

"My, what sharp teeth you have, grandma."

She'd spoken so softly that he'd almost missed her comment.

He shut his mouth with an audible click and sat up. "Are we playing games, princess?" The idea of playing games with the slim, delicate woman on the swing appealed to him.

Maybe there were possibilities here he hadn't considered. Maybe, despite his earlier conclusions, the princess was in the mood for some light flirting.

"Oh, I shouldn't think so."

Thinking he'd accidentally spoken aloud and she'd answered him, Hank blinked, at a loss for a reply.

But then she started to speak, and he took a deep breath.

Her foot trailed on the porch floor and she set the swing moving again, avoiding his gaze with a flicker of eyelashes, irritation still staining her smooth cheeks. "Playing games isn't my style."

"You don't know what you're missing, princess."

"Believe me, I know exactly what I'm missing." Wistful, sad, her husky voice sent a shiver over his skin. Unshed tears thickened the contralto. "And playing games with you wouldn't fill the void."

This time, she met his gaze, and Hank knew she was sending him a message beyond the truth she spoke.

Brushing away a pale pink petal that had somehow managed to cling to the hem of his trousers, he considered the situation.

Gillian Elliott was exactly what she appeared to be. A woman who needed more than he could offer.

Not his style at all.

He had nothing left to give a woman like her...even if he wanted to.

He knew he should walk away and leave her and her sleeping daughter alone on the porch.

That would be the smart thing to do. The prudent move.

But he'd never been prudent, not when there were more interesting things to do, and he was definitely more curious about Gillian Elliott than a prudent man would be.

So he wasn't altogether surprised to find himself taking one step over to the swing, where he placed one hand on each side of her.

Definitely not prudent to lean over her so close that they were nose to nose, so close that he couldn't escape her scent.

And heaven knew it wasn't smart to yield to that prickling aggression as he said, "Well, princess, since I don't scare the pants off you—" he gave the swing a small push "—and you aren't interested in playing games with me, I figure there's no reason at all that the three of us can't coexist right peaceably for a week or so, is there?"

Her wide, startled eyes met his.

Chapter Three

"Back up," Jilly said through clenched teeth. "You're in my space."

"Really?" His imitation of her earlier comment was dead on.

Jilly gripped the edge of the swing seat. She wouldn't move if it killed her. "If you think for one second that you're pushing my buttons—if you think you can bully me into staying here when I've already told you I don't intend to, you're—"

"I'm what, princess?" His nose actually bumped against hers and she wondered if her own eyes crossed the way his green-blue ones did. "I'm nuts? Rude? What?"

He gave the swing one more little push and the hard muscle of his thigh, a warm flex of male strength, brushed against her foot.

Jilly wished she'd kept her shoes on. She wished she'd stayed— Where? Home? That was the whole point. She hadn't been able to stay home. That was why Callie's suggestion had seemed like a gift from the gods, but now, thanks to this arrogant, pigheaded, pushy *cowboy*—

"Come on, princess. I'm waiting. What's the *mot juste*—"

She scowled at him.

"Yes, sugar," he said, nodding at her, "even we humble peasants know a word or two of French. So what's the right word for my behavior?" His smile was edgy, daring her.

"Oh, I have a *mot juste* or two for you."

"Yeah? Fire away. I'm listening, princess." He jiggled the swing seat. She couldn't understand how he could make her so angry so fast. She never lost her temper. "How about insufferable, obnoxious—"

He placed one warm finger against her lips and gave her a devilish smile. "That's your two."

Jerking her head back, she glared at him. "Irritating, annoying and insufferable."

"Finished?" He kissed the tip of her nose, nothing more than a butterfly's brush of his mouth over her skin, but her nyloned toes tingled, curled. Jake might be dangerous, but Hank Tyler was *dangerous*.

"Impudent," she said, her uncharacteristic anger making her slog doggedly on. At the moment, surrender had no place in her soul. "Cocky—"

"That's a good one," he encouraged, his grin impudent.

She didn't think the sparkle in his eyes came entirely from humor. Still, even though he seemed to be working a little too hard at it, she almost smiled. But some forgotten competitive instinct, or perhaps it was simply feminine pride, stirred, refused to acknowledge his cheeky, knowing male charm. She thought it was the fact that he knew she was resisting that made her dig in her heels harder. She lifted her chin and stared him down, ticking off the words on her fingers. "Obnoxious, repulsive—"

"No! Aw, princess. Not repulsive? That's terrible. I'm shocked. Truly, I am," he said, hanging his head and giving her such an appalled look from those dancing green-blue eyes that she laughed.

"And incorrigible," she muttered, anger draining away and leaving in its place a bubbling energy. Energy that had no name, no outlet. An energy that left her insides fizzing.

"How about friendly?"

"Too friendly, perhaps." She stared pointedly at his arms on either side of her.

He lifted his arms and stepped back. "There. See? I'm harmless. You win. You're tougher than I am, darlin'. Sure hope you don't go broadcasting to everybody how an itty-bitty thing like you had me shaking in my shoes."

"Hmm." She refused to give him the satisfaction of making her laugh again. "I saw exactly how petrified you were."

"Oh, you're an intimidating woman, Gillian Elliott, when you're in a temper," he said, all fake humility and overdone submissiveness as he widened his eyes, recoiling. "Lord knows, I'm a man with an exceptionally docile nature, but—"

"Docile?" Jilly pressed her lips tightly together. "You? *Docile?*"

"Of course." His expression was male smugness personified, but his slouch was too carefully casual, the glint in his eyes a shade too mischievous and filled with self-mockery. "You peeled a strip off my hide with all those fancy words you were tossing out."

"You had a few fancy words of your own. Even a couple of words that had more than one syllable," she acknowledged sweetly. "I'm impressed."

He slapped his forehead. "Lord, don't tell me I've been using four-dollar words? And in front of a lady like you? Shoot."

Jilly giggled. Only a small, almost-stifled sound, but it was too late. He'd heard her.

"See? You're not afraid of me. You know I'm not some wild-eyed—"

"I'm not too sure about the wild-eyed part."

"Maniac," he said, ignoring her interruption. Then, so fast she almost missed the change, he turned serious, his expression stripped of emotion.

In this mode, Hank Tyler kept her off balance. Or possibly it was his ability to make fun of himself. He was like summer lightning, brilliant, beautiful from a distance, but striking so fast that you were left sizzling and burning, never knowing where the danger had come from.

"So why couldn't we stay out of each other's way for this next week, Jilly? Couldn't we agree to a 'friendly' state of affairs between us for a limited time?"

"Could you possibly rephrase that? Particularly the state-of-affairs part?"

The fiend was laughing at her. If she'd had on her shoes, she would have yielded to temptation and kicked him. Hard.

"Sure." He placed his hand over his heart. "Your slightest wish, et cetera, et cetera. Isn't that how it goes?" A roar of cheers distracted his attention. He glanced toward the front of the house, then back at her.

But before he could continue, Jilly stopped him, curiosity and belated understanding trickling through her. "You did that on purpose, didn't you?"

"For the life of me, I don't know what you're talking about, princess," he drawled, leaning against one of the porch posts, giving her all the space she'd earlier demanded.

"Your clever little performance." Jilly wondered why it had taken her so long to realize that he'd been needling her. What she wanted to know now, though, was what his purpose had been. "You *wanted* to make me angry, didn't you?" Sliding Gracie out of her lap, Jilly stood up, walked shoeless across the porch to him, felt her nylons snag on the wood. "Why?"

Waiting for him to answer, Jilly heard the strumming notes of a guitar from the front yard, but she didn't let her gaze drift from his face.

He was silent for so long that she almost gave up.

Finally, with the guitar melody quivering in the air between them, he spoke, and his voice was so low she had to strain to hear him. "Because I figured you needed to know you could stay at the ranch while T.J. and Callie are gone if you wanted to. That you'd be safe here. With me." Restlessly, he turned, faced the sounds of the guitar. "And because I give in to impulses, Jilly. And maybe because I couldn't resist seeing if I could shake you out of that polite shell you live in." He threw her a teasing glance over his shoulder. "Are those enough reasons? Do you need more?"

"Yes, I think I need at least one more reason." She remembered the disturbing hint of darkness behind the humor, remembered that barely glimpsed pain. "I think you have an agenda of your own."

"Agenda? Lord, sugar, all these social-worker-type words."

She didn't answer, merely stood, waiting.

He sighed, and his shoulders hunched forward under the smooth material of his jacket as he braced his forehead against the post. "Devilment. Boredom. Whatever. Just because, Jilly. That's why." He sighed, straightened and pivoted to face her again. "Let's leave it at that, okay?"

"All right," she agreed. She'd hoped for a moment he might tell her the truth, but he hadn't. And that was all right. Whatever was going on inside Hank Tyler's head was his business, not hers. She shouldn't have pried. She had plenty of off-limits subjects of her own.

"Do you want an apology?" He smiled, crossed his arms and leaned against the post. "For inciting you to wrath? For kissing that stuck-up little nose of yours?"

Jilly felt all that fizzing inside rush to her face. "Kiss?"

His mouth firmly shut, he nodded.

"Oh, that. I scarcely noticed." She folded her arms.

"Really?" He didn't move a muscle.

"Really." She shrugged. "And I'm in charge of my temper. Not you. You don't owe me an apology."

"Oh, let me do the chivalrous thing and apologize, anyway, princess. For anything. For everything. I was out of line. I shouldn't have—" He stopped, fidgeted, straightened. Uncrossing his arms, he picked slowly at a splinter in the post, not meeting her eyes as he added, "But think about staying, all right?"

"I don't know." She plucked at one earring. The emeralds were hard, cold to her touch. "I can't see how the situation would work out. It's not what I expected."

"Oh? What did you expect, princess?"

"I—I don't know." Jilly rubbed her neck.

Hank's brief touch had been so—so *warm*.

She certainly hadn't expected to be so aware of the confounded man.

She hadn't expected to like his touch.

That was the danger.

The threat came from his casual ability to overpower the carefully balanced teeter-totter of her emotions, to make her think about—about *things*.

These last months she'd worked too hard to achieve the serenity she clung to like a life jacket. She valued it too much to toss it carelessly overboard simply because Hank Tyler had more oomph in one finger than her system was used to.

That serenity was a shield against idle curiosity and pity during the day. It was a protection against the fears and thoughts that hovered around her bed at night, so as he watched her with no expression on his suddenly hard face, she said again, "Whatever I expected, it wouldn't work. Both of us. Here." She shook her head vigorously. "Never."

"Of course it would." Hank stepped toward her, the shredded splinter falling beside him. "Nothing has changed from whatever you and Callie planned."

Jilly wanted to tell him everything had altered from the moment she'd gone to check on him as he lay under the oak tree, but she didn't.

"And if you wanted to take Sarah and Jake up on their offer," he said, "they would let Nicholas stay to keep Gracie company. She'd like that. It wouldn't be extra work for you. I'd keep an eye on him. On both of them."

"It's not the extra person. I like Nicholas," she said slowly, turning the idea over in her mind once more, adjusting to the idea of Hank Tyler being around for the whole week. "But I wouldn't cook." She tipped her chin up slightly, thinking it was important to establish boundaries early on with Hank Tyler.

"So who's asking you to?" He grinned. "My mama raised all her sons to fend for themselves in the kitchen. We can even run a dishwasher, princess. And I'm not used to being waited on, anyway."

"Hmm."

"Yes, *hmm* and really, I'm a nineties kind of guy. I can even mend my own socks."

Intrigued, she tilted her head. She didn't know anybody who mended socks anymore. "Do you?"

"Well, no. Mostly I pitch 'em and buy new ones. But I could sew up a sock if I needed to."

"Good for you." She clapped her hands.

"Hell, princess, I sew on buttons, and I've even been known to take an iron to a shirt. I'm self-sufficient. Self-reliant. All those good things."

"I'm impressed." Her face softened. There was more to Hank's self-sufficiency than he wanted her to see. But she saw. She'd caught that note of melancholy in spite of his self-mockery. "I understand. You're perfect," she teased.

"Of course." There was nothing modest in his smirk. "All we Tyler men are."

Her glance was reproachful, but she couldn't stop the smile that tugged her mouth up. "Modest, too, I see."

"Naturally." His grin almost made it to his eyes.

Rising over the guitar music, a roar of laughter came from the front yard and a rangy, whipcord-lean man poked his dark red head around the corner. "Hank! T.J. wants you around front. Right now. Or else."

"Hang on, Buck. I'll be there in a jiffy." He raised his hand palm out to stop the man from walking all the way to the porch. "My other brother. The oldest." He let his hand fall, and she felt the air brush against her.

"Make it fast, Hatty, or T.J.'ll kill us both." Buck disappeared.

"Hatty?" Jilly inquired politely.

"Sheesh. Brothers." Hank rolled his eyes. "My father loves baseball. Mama's crazy about music. Especially country singers."

"Yes?" Jilly had no idea where he was headed, but his look of chagrin tickled her. "And?"

"Hell, you know." He raked his fingers through his hair, ruffling it so hard golden-brown strands rose upright before he slicked them down impatiently. "People saddle their kids with the damnedest monikers."

"Hatty from Henry? I don't understand."

"Not Henry. Just Hank." He looked tormented.

Jilly almost relented, but by now she wanted to know. His embarrassment seemed so out of character. "All right. But I still don't get Hatty from Hank."

He shoved his hands into his pockets. "Uh, it was either Hank *Williams* Tyler. Or Hank *Aaron* Tyler. Music or baseball. Daddy begged. Mama gave in. But Daddy swears he paid for it over the years. I hope to hell he did. He should have," Hank concluded glumly.

"I see." Jilly bit her tongue to keep from giggling. "The initials. H.A.T. Thus, Hatty?"

"Yeah." He grimaced. "Thus, Hatty, and a few black eyes on all sides."

"Hmm."

Catching her expression, he laughed reluctantly. "*Brothers.* If you survive 'em, you're lucky."

"I wouldn't know. I don't have any brothers or sisters."

"Too bad."

"Perhaps." Jilly couldn't look at him as she said through her giggles, "But at least I didn't have to defend myself against nicknames. Hatty!"

"You know, princess, you have a sadistic streak under that cool, proper exterior, don't you?" He flicked her chin. "A real streak of mean down that pretty spine."

"Well, if I do, how unchivalrous of you to mention it," she said through her merriment.

Narrowing his eyes, he waited while her laughter subsided. "Sugar, you wouldn't have any trouble holding your own against anyone or anything, much less a pore ol' cowpoke like me. So why don't you stick with your original plan and stay the week at the ranch?"

She and Hank in the enclosed spaces of the ranch? For a week? For even a day? Impossible. Disaster in the making. She tried to get the words out, wanting to make him see what she sensed in her heart.

"Wait, Jilly. Don't say no. Not on my account. I swear on a stack of Bibles I'll stay out of your way. I'll keep the kids busy. But just don't let Callie and T.J. down, okay?"

"You don't play fair." She looked down at the earring that she'd worried loose from its backing. The emeralds and diamonds glittered, winked against her hand.

Gracie stirred, sat up. "Mommy?" She rubbed her eyes. "Are we still doing Callie's wedding?" She looked around, scrambled to her feet as she heard the music and shouts. "Oh, good. I'll go find Nickels."

Bowing, Hank opened the screen door for her. "Say good night, Gracie."

"G'night," she called as she skidded around the corner of the house.

"I know. Corny, but it was always Mama's little night-time joke with us boys." He shrugged.

"Hank," Jilly began uncertainly, "you'd be better off without Gracie and me underfoot. It's your home."

"Was. Hasn't been mine for years. Buck and I sold our shares. Now the ranch is T.J.'s and Callie's." He wiggled the door invitingly. "Don't you want to shower them with roses and gardenias? Say goodbye to them? Callie will be wondering where you are." He opened the door wider, gesturing her toward it. "You can tell me later what you've decided. But for now, what do you say we mosey on around front and join the rest of the crowd?"

Once again Jilly sensed that he wanted her company, and that puzzling awareness troubled her, jolted her into looking at him as a man.

Now, waiting patiently for her, he waggled both eyebrows in time with the door. "Come on," he coaxed. "One baby step forward. *Good* girl," he said as her foot moved.

"Oh, hush," she grumbled. "I haven't been a girl for years. Besides it's not politically correct to call women girls anymore. You should know that."

"Babes, then?" he inquired innocently, his eyes dancing.

"Just be quiet. You're in enough trouble. And I haven't agreed to stay, you know."

"Right." He gestured toward the front. "But you will. Come on. I promise I'll behave."

"I doubt it," Jilly said gloomily. "I don't think 'behave' is in your genes."

He didn't glance down at his slacks, but the impulse showed in the way his eyes held hers steadily even though his eyebrows rose.

"Don't say another word."

"Me?" His eyebrows zoomed a notch higher, indicating complete innocence.

"You."

It would have been easier to ignore him if he didn't make her laugh.

Jilly slipped on her heels and walked out the door with Hank at her side, his long strides shortening to match hers.

He slipped his hand under her elbow. His forearm lay snugly against hers, firm, *there*, its strength implicit. "You might trip," he said.

"I might," she agreed, letting his hand stay where it was. "Anything could happen."

"There you go, princess, getting my hopes up." He stood for a moment laughing at her, and then he strolled leisurely toward the festivities in the front yard.

When he hesitated at the corner of the house and took a deep breath, seeming to steel himself, Jilly curled her fingers around his; it would have been cruel not to extend the small comfort.

T.J. and Callie waved them forward. Callie's pale pink suit glowed against the light gray fabric of T.J.'s sleeve.

Hank tucked her arm close to his chest as he strolled forward, nonchalance in every step. "Not too late to give the bride a kiss, is it?" Sunny goodwill radiated from him.

"What do you think we've been waiting for?" T.J. grumbled. "Callie said she wouldn't leave until she kissed you goodbye."

"Well, hell, Thomas J., why didn't you say so earlier? I thought you needed help cutting the cake. I've been looking forward all day to giving Callie her goin'-away, married-lady kiss."

His square face was open, amiable, nothing hidden behind its good humor. His performance was so perfect that Jilly wondered how he'd fooled people all this time. Couldn't anyone else see the tightness at the corners of his eyes? The clench of his free hand as it lay casually in his pocket?

Although Hank gave her an apologetic smile, Jilly wasn't sure he even saw her as he dropped their joined hands and walked up to Callie, giving her a big hug before sweeping her into a mock-passionate kiss that bent her back over his arm as the crowd around them clapped and hooted.

"Better watch those two, T.J.," a white-haired man called out.

A skinny man in a woven straw cowboy hat whipped off his hat, sending it skyward as he yelled, "Hey, Callie, you sure you don't want to change your mind?"

"That's enough, buddy," T.J. said, tapping Hank on the head. "Even if you are my little brother, I draw the line at twenty-minute farewells with my bride."

"Spoilsport," Hank complained. "We were just warming up." He grabbed a glass of champagne from one of the caterer's serving trays and extended the glass toward them. "Congratulations, Thomas Jefferson. I couldn't be prouder of you—even if you are too bossy for your own good. You're a good brother. I love you. And I wish you and Callie and Charlie all the happiness in the world. You deserve it." He raised the glass. Sunlight turned the amber liquid into shimmering gold. "To my brother and his wife. To two good people. May their union be blessed."

"Hear, hear," someone called out. Glasses lifted, clinked.

And then the afternoon erupted into pink and white as petals drifted all around Callie and T.J.

Off to the side of the front steps, Gracie whirled and flung petals with abandon, showering everyone near her with fragrance and color.

Through the haze of her tears, Jilly wondered if she was still the only one who saw the overly careful way Hank returned his empty glass to a nearby table. Was she the only person in this whole crowd of his friends and relatives who saw the dazed look on his face, who saw behind the mask of his banter?

Their blindness angered her, but it shouldn't have; it wasn't any of her concern. But, oh, they were so oblivious to the pain she saw in Hank Tyler, and they were his *family*. They should have *seen*.

Drawn to him in spite of herself, Jilly reached out her hand and turned abruptly, clumsily, toward him, stumbling against a woman. Catching herself on the arm of the woman, she said, "Excuse me." Regaining her balance, she found herself looking down into the round face of Bea Tyler, Hank's mother.

"Careful, sugar," the woman said absently, her gaze following Hank. "Don't want to ruin that pretty green dress."

Smile lines crinkled out from the older woman's hazel eyes, crumpled the soft skin of her mouth. Hers was the face of a woman given to smiling a lot, the face a record of a woman who had sought out happiness and the silver lining at every opportunity.

It was also the face of a mother worried about her son.

Like his mother, Jilly watched as Hank drifted away from the crowd, slowing his stride for a moment to talk to Buck, to Sarah and Jake. Sunlight touched his hair, glowed around him as he moved through the swirl of faces.

He turned with everyone else to cheer as Callie and T.J. raced for Callie's car in another flurry of petals and huzzahs.

All the easy grace of his movements had flown. He moved like the walking wounded.

"Damn," Bea whispered. "Damn, damn."

Slipping quietly away, Jilly went to find her own child.

At that moment Jilly decided she would stay, as she'd agreed, at the ranch.

With Gracie.

With Hank.

Because she knew, deep down at the most elemental level, that he was a man who needed noise and people around him.

At least for a while.

And, after all, Jilly muttered to herself as she went in search of Gracie, Nicholas and Nicholas's parents, she didn't have a lot of options.

In spite of the way her skin warmed to his most casual touch, he would be no threat to the emotional balance she'd achieved. Hank Tyler was in love with his sister-in-law.

And Callie had never known. Had never seen past Hank's teasing mask.

He'd kept his secret from everyone except his mother.

And herself, Jilly realized as she saw him lean against a gunmetal gray car, his head tipped back to the sky where the morning's clouds gathered again. His eyes were shut, his mouth a thin, tight line.

The golden afternoon was over.

By nighttime, it would be raining again.

Jilly was bone-weary by the time the full force of the rain pounded against the roof of the ranch house.

Hank had only nodded when she'd stammeringly informed him that she'd changed her mind once more. "Good. I'm glad," he'd said and disappeared with the last of the stragglers into the darkness just before the rain began.

She had no idea whether he intended to sleep in the ranch house or in one of the barns or outbuildings. For all she knew, he was going to take care of the livestock in his suit. She told herself it didn't matter.

But she couldn't help checking the windows for the shine of a flashlight or lantern in all the dark.

Nicholas had been allowed to stay for a "day or two only," and Gracie was happily ordering him around. Her nightgown dragged behind her on the wooden floor.

"Here, Nickels, you can have this side of the bed. And I will let you sleep with my doll baby." She held out a bedraggled, half-bald doll in a rhinestone-spangled dress.

"Nope." Nicholas scrambled onto the bed. "Brought Froggie." Rear end tipped to the ceiling, he doubled over to the floor, clinging with one hand to the bed as he dragged a duffel bag toward him. Under his "morpher fighter"

T-shirt, white cotton briefs flashed as he straightened with a satisfied grunt.

Jilly had a moment's panic as she wondered whether or not Froggie was real. Froggie was green, huge and furry, sitting between the two children as if at any moment he would speak.

After giving both children a kiss and hug, Jilly had to plant a kiss on Froggie.

"Good night, Nicholas, Gracie. Go to sleep. You, too, Froggie."

She wandered through the house, liking the homey spaces, the large living room, the worn oak table in the kitchen.

A hundred and eighty degrees different from her Naples house, this home had a comfortable shabbiness at its edges, a sense of identity.

Trailing her fingers over the rectangular dining room table, she let the sounds of the old home move against her, fill her and push away the emptiness of nighttime.

The creak of wood. The steady drumming of rain.

A distant boom of thunder.

For a long time she stood in the kitchen, absorbing the sounds, letting her mind drift over the last months.

Time enough to deal with the past in the coming days.

The kitchen door banged against the wall, Jilly jumped and Hank stomped into the kitchen. His wet boots squelched with each step. He shoved off a battered cowboy hat, slapping its wet felt against his thighs. Water splattered everywhere. "Sorry," he said wearily as he saw the spray of raindrops. "Cruddy night out there. I'll clean it up," he added as Jilly hunted for paper towels.

Shining with beads of water, his hair was wet, dark. His face was rainwashed, empty of energy and humor as he yanked off the sopping boots and tossed them into the utility room off the kitchen. They thumped against the wall.

One more night sound.

Barefoot, he slouched in front of her. From the bottoms of his faded jeans, water dripped in small, quiet plops onto the tile floor. Lifting the tail of a bleached-out plaid shirt, he wiped his face dry.

Shining damp in the light, his belly was flat, smooth.

She meant to look away. She never intended to let her gaze linger on that tanned sweep of rain-slick skin.

But it was late, and she was tired and confused.

Dropping the shirttail, he saw her glance slide away and he paused, motionless as he looked at her, his eyes narrowed against the kitchen light, focusing on her.

The sunshine cowboy had disappeared into the night and rain, leaving only a man with glittering green eyes in a lined, exhausted face staring at her across the width of an old kitchen table.

Chapter Four

Outside, its drops splattering against the windows, the rain had settled into a steady thrumming on the roof.

Inside, water dripped quietly from the edges of his clothes onto the tiles, drizzled in cold rivulets down the back of his neck. Bone-weary and chilled to every inch of his aching body, Hank stood motionless in a puddle of muddy water.

The kitchen was so quiet that he heard the altered rhythm of Jilly's breathing, her tiny gasp as he let his shirt fall back in place.

That hushed sound was a whispering touch along his wet skin, and he shivered as if she'd actually breathed against it and slid her narrow palms over his belly, pressed her long, warm fingers against his rib cage.

Heat whipped through him.

Stunned, he couldn't move, couldn't speak. Sharp, unexpected, it was a scorpion sting that streaked down his nerve endings, leaving him burning in its wake.

Looking into her startled, wary eyes, he was swamped with a craving to pick her up and carry her down the hall to his room, slam the door and let the drumming of the rain echo in the pulse of their bodies, let the rain and darkness enclose them in a cocoon of touch and sound.

Oh, he *wanted*.

Wanted to taste the softness of her mouth.

Wanted to forget. For an hour or two.

The warm rush of blood beat so fast through him that his fingertips tingled with cold and heat and the need to touch her.

Not thinking, only responding to that need, he lifted his hand and saw the pupils of her eyes dilate and darken in instinctive, feminine invitation. An invitation he knew she wouldn't offer knowingly.

Hank let his hand fall to his side.

And she spoke at the same time in a breathy, panicked voice. "No," she said, shaking her head slowly, slowly from side to side. "No." And the sound, a movement of air and breath, stirred in the room.

"No," he agreed but couldn't stop staring at her, couldn't stop the hammering in his blood. Looking at her, seeing the reflection of himself in her shocked eyes made him hungry, made him ache, but it was a change from the hollowness that had been inside him all day. It was the hunger he'd sensed earlier and, like a fool, had decided wouldn't be a problem.

He shifted uncomfortably, saw the way her eyes unconsciously followed his movements.

And everywhere that soft blue gaze lingered, a heavy heat gathered.

His throat grew tight.

Idiotic to believe for one cotton-pickin' second that she could ease for a moment or two the emptiness deep inside him.

Damned stupid to think having Jilly here would help him get past this crummy day that he'd faked his way through.

He shouldn't have tried to tease her into changing her mind and staying. What had he been thinking?

T.J.'s bourbon had obviously pickled what remained of his brain and left it worthless.

The wind slapped a sheet of rain against the window fronting the porch. Jilly blinked, stirred, and with her movement, the grass-green material of her skirt tightened around the smooth stretch of her legs.

It drew his attention to that long curve of hip and thigh.

And he was aware of a different heat now, slow and thick.

Hell, he'd known he liked looking at her, liked breathing in the scent of her, but he'd liked *looking* at a lot of women.

Looking was never a problem. A woman was one of nature's blessings. At least, that's what he'd always believed. And he was a man who was genuinely appreciative of nature's gifts.

As for *liking* a woman, well, shoot, that hadn't been a problem, either. He liked women a whole, heapin' bunch.

Liking them had its own pleasures, its own rules.

He'd always played fair, though. That had been one of the rules. Playing fair kept him real careful to keep emotions out of the one-plus-one equation. For him, one plus one would always add up to two. Two distinct individuals, two people. That blending of two separate souls and spirits into one was not for him.

He'd lost that chance.

Not worth whining about, though. It was just the way things worked out sometimes.

So he'd played it safe. Been up front about the limits. About his rules, his boundaries. Had played the game safe, fair, and had been real, real careful on all levels.

And no one had been hurt.

There had been no complications, no problems. But now—

He cleared his throat.

The woman in front of him with the look of someone whose emotions had leaped out of a cave and surprised her, well, she was turning into a complication.

Maybe it was the too-aware look in those cautious eyes. Something awfully seductive about a woman who looked at a man the way Jilly had looked at him, with that unconscious yearning in her eyes and her mouth opening, her lips going all soft and full.

Or maybe it was the sleek swoop of dark brown hair sliding against her smooth cheeks, the high curve on those cheekbones turning rosy as each moment passed and he couldn't look away from her, couldn't get his fill of watching the play of light and shadow against her hair, her skin.

The slide of soft fabric over her hips, legs.

The curve of her breasts under the green fabric.

Lord knew he liked looking at this woman.

Trouble was, though, during this nightmare of a day, he'd discovered he liked *her,* Gillian Elliott. The person inside the package.

She intrigued him, touched him at a level he hadn't reckoned on with that glimpse of vulnerability he'd seen peeking out from behind her princess elegance.

And that felt entirely too personal. Because it was more than the image she presented that attracted him. More than smooth skin and curves.

He shook his head and drops of water sprayed the floor. Several droplets flew against the green of her dress along the slope of her left breast, glued the thin fabric to her skin.

A tiny point pebbled under the drop as it slid over the tip of her breast. Watching that tiny shivering point, Hank couldn't breath for a moment. And then, as she inhaled, the droplet trembled, disappeared.

"Don't look at me like that." Her hand was at the base of her throat, and he saw the faint flutter of her pulse where her fingers spread open. "I don't want you to look at me, not like that."

Her words released him from that sense of being cata-pulted back into the gawky sexuality of a fifteen-year-old, where every waking second was charged with testosterone awareness. Where everything was brighter, hotter, turbo-charged.

"Like how, princess?" He swept his hair back, dried his hands down his soaked jeans, and breathed deeply. With each steadying rush of oxygen to his brain, his thinking cleared, and he reminded himself that there were two kids who might or might not be sound asleep down the hall. "How am I looking at you?"

"As if you want to...you know. Flirting."

He laughed and the tension eased inside him. That heat seeped away, reminding him he was soaking wet. Not as good as a cold shower, but it would do for the moment. "Flirting? Is that what we were doing? I was looking at you the way a man looks at a woman he'd like to go to bed with, to put it bluntly. I'd call it a little bit more than *flirting*, sugar. Wouldn't you? Or is that the *polite* way of referring to what I was thinking?"

"Whatever you want to call it, don't look at me that way." Moving her hands from her throat, she fastened them around her waist as if—he told himself what he wanted to believe—as if she was afraid she would reach out to him. "Please. I'm not—"

"Not what, sugar?" He threw the words over his shoulder, watching her casually as he took out a cup from the cupboard, filled it with faucet water and stuck it into the microwave. He closed the microwave door gently and tried to ignore the tiny vibrations in his hand.

Not Callie Jo, Jilly almost said, catching the words in time. "Not interested, that's what," she said instead. "I told you. I don't play games. And you don't do anything but play."

She watched the flick of his agile fingers against the microwave number pad as he set the timer.

"True." He leaned against the counter and grinned at her, his teeth a flash of white in the beard-shadowed contours of his face. It was the same grin he'd worn all afternoon, the careless, lighthearted smile of a man with nothing more important on his mind than a casual flirtation between consenting adults, but Jilly recognized the megawatt smile for the mask it was. "But you can't blame a man for appreciating what's in front of him, can you?"

"I haven't decided."

He stretched his arms out beside him along the top of the counter. "Besides, princess, I sure did like the way *you* appreciated me. Feel free to appreciate me all you want. I don't mind."

"How very generous of you." She shook her head. "You know something, Hank Aaron Tyler?"

"What's that, sugar?"

"You're not a—a restful man to be around."

"Thanks." His grin widened, but he didn't move. "I sure wouldn't want to be a *restful* man."

Jilly felt the blush creeping up her neck and turned abruptly away from him. "You're impossible." She pressed her palms against her hot cheeks as she walked past the table, away from him, away from the tumult of feelings stirring inside her.

"Not always," he said so meekly that she stumbled as she walked toward the hall leading to the bedrooms. "It all depends. Sometimes, sugar, I'm very—possible."

The burr of roughness under his placid tone ruffled the hairs along her arms. "You don't give up, do you?"

"Nope. Never found much point in quitting the battle before it's won."

"I see. Men. Women. It's a battle?" Jilly wondered if he ever regretted yielding the field to T.J., wondered if Hank ever regretted not letting Callie know his feelings. Wondered exactly how hard he'd had to work to keep his secret. "A war to the death?"

"Just a pleasant skirmish, princess. One where every-body wins. If they play the game with the right—" the lift of a thick brown eyebrow was nothing but innocence "—weapons."

"I give up. I'm waving a white flag." Ignoring the quiver in her abdomen, Jilly stalked down the hall toward the room where she was sleeping. "You win. I'm speechless."

"Cat got your tongue?"

She stopped. She shouldn't have.

"Lucky cat."

Jilly wouldn't touch that comment with a fifteen-foot pole, much less a ten-footer. There was absolutely no sense in encouraging the man. He generated enough turmoil all by himself. Encouragement was the last thing the big lunk-head needed. The old saying about giving someone an inch and he would take a mile was an understatement when ap-plied to the man slouched so serenely at the counter, so she fled the field of battle. "Good night." She drew on all her skill to make the two syllables sound indifferent, nothing more than social discourse.

"Good night, sugar. Parting is such sweet sorrow and all that."

All the way down the hall, she felt his amused gaze right between her shoulder blades, his amusement mocking her counterfeit indifference.

But he was still leaning against the counter and grinning at her when she glanced back at him over her shoulder.

"Sleep tight." There was nothing but delighted wicked-ness in his eyes as he drawled, "And sweet dreams, sugar. I'm planning to have a very *restful* night myself."

Jilly wished she had her shoes on. She would have pitched one right at his smiling face. "It's been a long day. I'm sure I'll sleep well. And dreamlessly."

His long, drawn-out "Aw, princess, what a shame" ech-oed down the hall after her, and like the Cheshire cat he just smiled. The image of that wide smile hovered in the air behind her as she went inside the bedroom where the children were and closed the door.

Back to back, Gracie and Nicholas were sound asleep, Gracie's fist curled tightly into her doll's hair, Nicholas's arm squeezed over Froggie's no-neck.

Securing the blanket and sheet under the mattress, Jilly sighed. Callie had been trying to do her a favor, but the situation was untenable.

Like an electrical appliance that vibrated silently to the touch, conveying its energy to the toucher, Hank Tyler agitated her, made her edgy, made her think of things she was better off not thinking about.

Things like touching, for instance, she scolded herself as she adjusted the shades at the window. And the way a man could make a woman feel all mushy and warm inside with nothing more than a teasing, knowing look.

Things that made her feel disloyal to a husband who had sacrificed so much to give her everything he thought she wanted, who had adored her and told her so, every day, every night.

She didn't understand the sense of guilt gnawing at her. She'd loved Larry, too. Of course she had. He had been the kind of husband little girls dreamed of when they imagined fairy-tale lives and princes as husbands.

But princes and princesses didn't live happily ever after. Not in real life they didn't. Anybody who paid attention to the news knew that. Lingering at the window, staring out at the shimmer of rain in the darkness, she remembered other days, other hopes. The fragile hopes of a small girl who believed that the story was over when the book was closed on the last page.

Leaning against the cool pane of glass, she thought about fantasies. About reality. She thought about all that waiting around for someone else to solve your problems, and about princesses who had no life of their own until the prince rode up on his white charger.

She rubbed her aching forehead against the glass. All that waiting for all those Sleeping Beauties. Wasted lives. Wasted time.

She wasn't a little girl anymore who thought happily-ever-after was guaranteed when the prince showed up on his white horse. Or in a fancy car. Reality was a whole different kettle of fish, as the proverb went, and not necessarily worse.

Remembering the focused intensity of Hank Tyler's eyes on Callie and T.J., Jilly knew that reality had its own attractions. The fleeting, wistful thought curled around the edges of her consciousness as she turned away from her contemplation of the night and leaned over to kiss Gracie.

For a real-live girl-child, fairy tales could be as constricting as old-time corsets used to be. She touched the bald patches in the plastic hair of Gracie's doll.

And little girls grew up to be women who could feel restricted, strangled. She didn't want that kind of existence for her daughter.

What did she want for herself?

For an instant her fingers stilled against the cotton-candy hair of the doll.

What did she *want?*

A shiver slipped down her spine, right down to her toes, curling them. And then, straightening, she shoved the thought back into the darkness it deserved. It was as much a betrayal as her unexpected response to Hank Tyler.

Jilly opened the door, peeked down the hall to the empty kitchen. Feeling like a sneak, she tiptoed down the hall to the room where she was sleeping. And was so relieved not to encounter her tormentor that she was embarrassed.

A few minutes later, hearing him in the kitchen as she listened for sounds like a thief in the night, she managed to avoid Hank during a quick trip to the bathroom as she readied herself for bed.

Standing in the bathroom with her hand on the door-knob, Jilly started to giggle. The picture of herself skulking around the house was ridiculous. She knew she must look like a fool. But the urge to hide was stronger than the image of herself lurking behind doors, listening with every cell in her body for sounds of the presence of a rascal who could unnerve her with a grin and a look.

And so she stayed there in the bathroom, huddled behind the door and torn between wanting to let out whoops of laughter and a sense of abject humiliation, until she was sure the hall was clear.

Until she was sure she would be safe.

Moments later, lying in the old-fashioned double bed with its iron head- and footboard, she clutched the sheet beneath her and wanted to weep with frustration and loneliness. She didn't understand the hot tears seeping from under her eyelids. It was all Hank Aaron Tyler's fault, she thought, thumping the mattress with a doubled-up fist.

She hadn't felt like this even at the funeral. Even on that terrible day with tears bottled up and Gracie silent at her side, she'd been clear about her emotions, known what she was feeling. She'd known what her obligations were. Known what she was supposed to do.

But ever since she'd gone to help Hank, he'd confused her. He made her think. Worst of all, he made her feel agitated, unsettled. Muddled.

She didn't want to think. She certainly didn't want this whirlpool of emotions churning inside her.

It had to be the aftershock of the wedding. Certainly the day had brought back memories of her own wedding, memories of Larry. Turning over and drawing her knees up to her chest, Jilly smoothed the empty space beside her over and over, her palm finding no comfort in the sweep of fabric against her skin.

The bed was too big, too empty.

And she couldn't put a name to what she wanted.

Drifting to sleep with one lumpy pillow under her head and the other clutched as tightly to her as Gracie's doll, Jilly rubbed her hot, damp face against the pillow, determined not to let Hank's laughing, mocking figure trespass on her dreams.

He had no place in her thoughts, her dreams. She had no place in this house. And yet she needed to stay. For a few days. Only until her lawyer had straightened out the mess regarding her accounts that he'd called her about. She brought the pillow closer to her.

But...

Hank could be a problem. The man had an uncanny ability to flip the switch on her emotions.

Down the hall, from the bathroom, she heard the gurgle of pipes, the rush of water from the shower and she stirred restlessly.

Watching the shadows move across the pale walls, she finally admitted that the problem wasn't Hank. The confusion came from inside her, and she didn't know how to deal with it. Except by staying away from him.

Soft footsteps hesitated outside her door.

A shiver ran over her skin. She lifted her head, turning to that muffled sound.

"G'night, princess." The footsteps faded, then from a bedroom at the end of the hall near the master bedroom, a door shut quietly.

The sheet burned her skin. Restless and tense, she turned irritably, stuffing the edge of the pillow under her chin as she shut her eyes.

Hank Tyler's smile floated on her closed lids.

She opened her eyes to the cool darkness and silence of the bedroom where the rain still pattered against the window, silvery drops sliding down the glass.

As if drawn toward each other magnetically, two drops merged into one and drifted down the window in a long, slow slide.

Her silk nightgown slithered up her legs as she turned again, away from the window, and shut her eyes determinedly.

She might not be able to ignore Hank Tyler as Callie had promised, but there was no reason she couldn't avoid him. It was a big house, a big ranch. There was lots of space for her and Gracie to get lost in. She probably wouldn't even see Hank after tonight. Surely he would be busy doing whatever cowboys did. Surely he wouldn't be in and out of the ranch house, giving her those looks, provoking her with his sly jabs.

Surely she should have had better sense, Jilly concluded glumly the next morning as Gracie and Nicholas came somersaulting onto the bed and Hank stared down at her from the doorway.

"Don't you have work to do? Cowboy stuff?" she asked groggily.

"Sure." He ambled in, the heels of his boots thunking on the floor. Shoving a dented cowboy hat off his face, he raked a hand through his sweat-damp hair.

"Well, why aren't you doing it?" Jilly tried to scrunch down under the sheet, but Gracie and Nicholas were jumping up and down and flopping spread-eagle on either side of her.

Facing her, Hank sprawled in a chair in the corner of the room. "Been there. Done that." He stretched out his legs. "For a while, at least. Came in for breakfast. These guys begged me to fix them a cowboy breakfast."

"What?" Frantically trying to wrestle the sheet free of the two wriggling children, Jilly pulled it up to her chin. Between them, they had her wrapped tighter than a mummy. Even the shape of her kneecap was clearly visible, and she didn't even want to think about what other body parts were making themselves known.

"Breakfast. Eggs. Toast. Grits and ham. You know. Food."

"Breakfast? How late is it?" She grabbed her wrist-watch and held it close to her face, peering with disbelief at the slender black hour hand.

"Well, you said you weren't cooking," Hank said reasonably, rising and snagging Nicholas just before the boy's head met the metal knob at the corner of the headboard.

"But—" she shook the watch "—it's five-thirty in the morning."

"Yep, that it is, princess. Got to get up early and get a head start on the day, you know." With his index finger, he freed Gracie's foot where its every movement wound the sheet more snugly against Jilly. "Go back to sleep." His finger brushed Jilly's arm, caught against the drooping spaghetti strap of her French-made nightgown. He glanced at her quickly but didn't say anything. The suddenly intense look in his green-blue eyes said everything for him. "I'll corral these hooligans for a while. Put 'em to work. Right, monkeys?" He grabbed the back of Nicholas's T-shirt, helping him out of the tangle of sheets and blankets.

"Yep." Yawning, Nicholas rolled to his feet and scratched his skinny, T-shirted belly.

Gracie scratched her rounded one. "Yep. See you, Mommy." She marched past the bed. "Me and Nickles gonna be cowboys."

"Wait," Jilly croaked, her voice scratchy and sleep-filled. "Just a second, guys. Gracie, Nicholas, you need to put on work clothes!" Holding the sheet in front of her, Jilly slid her feet onto the cool floor while her daughter waggled her rear end out the door. "Gracie Jean, wait!"

"Don't worry. We'll find duds." With a seesaw motion, Hank settled his hat on his head and headed for the door. "We should be back around noon. Or thereabouts. Depends on how hard these cowpokes work." Giving a tip of his hat to Jilly, Hank winked at the kids. "They'll be fine. Long as they don't go messing with the bulls."

"No!" Jilly called, knowing he was razzing her, but not liking the idea of Gracie and Nicholas roaming loose among horned beasts of doubtful disposition. But of course

Hank wouldn't... Would he? Clutching pillow and sheet to her breasts, she lurched to her feet.

"Nice duds of your own, princess." Hank's gaze trailed over her bare feet, up her thigh to the streak of silky black bodice revealed by the gap between pillow and sheet. "Sure wish I didn't have chores waiting for me." He shooed the kids out the door with a wry glance behind him.

"Wait! We haven't discussed—"

The door slammed behind them.

Half a second too late, her pillow thudded against it. She groaned. The kitchen sink would be filled with greasy skillets. There would be pots with congealed lumps of sickeningly white grits. She didn't want to think about the stove. The prospect was enough to make anyone gag and go back to bed.

She fumed. He was impossible. How anybody could survive a day with the man, much less a week or two, was anybody's guess. He'd test the limits of a saint.

Caught between annoyance and amusement, she ripped back the sheets and shook them. At best, the kitchen would be a disaster area. At worst, they would have to call in a bulldozer. She'd cooked with Gracie before. With Gracie and Nicholas both "helping," Hank would have had his hands full.

Flipping the bedspread over the neatly straightened sheets, Jilly decided that fair was fair. They'd cooked. She'd clean up. This time. But if they decided to have cowboy breakfasts again, everybody would have to pitch in.

She removed her nightgown and flung it into a yanked-open drawer, then struggled into linen slacks and a long-sleeved cotton shirt over a camisole, her sleep-numbed fingers fumbling with snaps, buttons and zipper. Leaving the top three buttons of the silvery gray shirt undone, she took a deep breath and left the bedroom, ready to face whatever was skulking in the kitchen.

Filled with noble forbearance and tolerance and prepared to forgive the threesome even glued-on egg, she stumbled bleary-eyed into the kitchen.

The sight of the sparkling kitchen should have filled her with joy. But it was exasperation that twanged her nerve endings.

Unable to vent her smugness, she felt deprived. And she didn't understand that, either.

But it didn't seem fair somehow that Hank had already put in a morning's work, fixed breakfast and cleaned up afterward.

All that energy was like a slap in the face. Almost as if he was challenging her in some indefinable way, she thought grumpily as she took a mug of coffee out to the porch and stared into the distance, leaving the accusing cleanliness of the kitchen behind her.

His message was obvious.

She knew how he saw her. He made it clear every time he called her *princess*.

Funny. Larry had called her that, too. Reverently, though, not with that slightly needling drawl of Hank's. Larry had never needled, never teased her. She winced as a too-quick sip of coffee burned her mouth.

Let Hank Tyler think what he wanted to. It didn't matter. He didn't know anything about her. She opened the screen door and pitched the rest of the coffee onto the hydrangea bushes near the step.

He'd cooked an enormous breakfast for himself. For her child. For her child's friend. And acted as if it were as easy as falling off a log. No mess. No fuss. Knowing what she thought she did about him, she decided he was definitely goading her.

Carrying the empty cup back to the kitchen, Jilly tapped its edge lightly against her teeth, thinking. She'd said she wouldn't cook.

But he would learn she always paid her debts.

She looked out the long window that opened onto the wraparound screened porch. Pink and pearling up through the mist that lay over the fields as far as she could see, the sun rose low on the horizon.

It was Sunday.

She had time. Good grief, it was only six in the morning. She had hours.

If that showboating cowboy thought he could... Jilly opened the freezer door, scanned the contents with an experienced eye. Grimly she extracted a package of frozen chicken.

A woman was entitled to change her mind when the situation called for it.

When Gracie and Nicholas came slamming through the screen door into the kitchen, Gracie's face was stormy, mud-streaked and teary. Nicholas managed to look overwhelmed and stubborn at the same time.

Bringing up the rear, Hank shrugged his shoulders. Green and blue plaid rippled over his shoulders with his movements. "Tired and hungry. I think," he said, shaking his head.

For a second, she thought he meant himself, but then Gracie buried her face against Jilly's leg.

With two long strides, Hank was past her, a rueful expression lifting his mouth. "They're all yours, sugar."

"Coward," Jilly muttered to his retreating back.

"Nope, just smart enough to know when I'm out of my league. I'm only a man, after all." He vanished through the arch between the kitchen and utility room.

Jilly heard boots banging onto the floor, his sigh of relief.

Nicholas tugged at her pants leg. "I didn't do nothin' to her."

She wrapped an arm around him and lifted Gracie, hugging her. "What's wrong, troops?"

Heading past her once more, this time toward the hall and the bathroom, Hank walked behind her, leaving a faint scent of fresh air, horses and man in his wake. "Sorry," he murmured into her ear. "I probably kept them out too long. We'll go out somewhere and grab a bite to eat soon as I shower off the mud and glop. Or we can open a can of soup. There should be something edible in cans."

Jilly ignored the impulse that almost made her turn her head to inhale the air he'd just walked through, to take that clean, healthy scent deep into her lungs. Instead, she concentrated on her daughter, whose face was burrowing insistently into her neck and chest. "Oh, doodlebug, didn't you and Nicholas have a nice morning?"

"Yes. But not all the time." Gracie twisted, leaned down to Nicholas. "And girls can *too* be cowboys 'cause Hank said so. And if you don't b'lieve me, you're not my friend, Nickels, and we *won't* play anymore. So there." She pressed her face into Jilly's neck. "Nickels doesn't b'lieve girls can do cowboy stuff. Just fishing stuff." Her small chest heaved with a sob. "And I'm gonna be a cowboy if he is." By now, her sturdy little body shook with sobs. "But I can't make my behind stay in the saddle, and I can't make the rope go around *anything!* And Nickels *can.*"

"My Jake papa taught me." A man of few words, Nicholas climbed up onto a kitchen chair and drummed his feet against the rungs.

Laying his head flat on the table so that he was looking at Jilly sideways, he smiled, a smile of such pure male satisfaction that Jilly bit her lip to keep from laughing.

Nicholas was going to be a pistol when he grew up. Regarding him thoughtfully, Jilly wondered if all the males in the area were born with killer smiles or if there was something in the water they drank.

She made a mental note to make sure that Gracie was nowhere around when that miniature male developed an interest in something besides fishing, horses and cows.

"My Jake papa can do *everything*. And I can, too, because he learns me how."

"I don't care *anything* about your Jake papa," Gracie wailed, twisting in Jilly's arms and wrapping her arms tightly around Jilly's neck. "And my daddy didn't like horses and cows and stuff like that. But he's not here, or he'd show me anyway! You're mean, Nickels and I hate you, so there!"

"I am not mean. But I am real sorry Gracie's papa can't teach her like my Jake papa does. That's all," the boy said, flopping his head away from them. "I din't mean to hurt your feelings, Gracie," he mumbled, not looking at Gracie, whose sobs had subsided to hiccups. "You could practice roping and riding. I want me and you to be friends."

Gracie's death-grip on Jilly's neck loosened as Gracie peered over one chubby arm at Nicholas.

"And I want to go home," Nicholas said. "I want my mommy and I want Jake." His shoulder twitched and a pitiful gulp came from the region of his diminutive chest. "I want to go home! I'm homesick!" Another heart-tearing gulp.

Rocking Gracie in her arms, wishing she had another set so that she could wrap her arms around Nicholas, too, Jilly said, "It's been a long day, hasn't it, honey? Tell you what. Why don't you go knock on the bathroom door, and see if Hank can make room in there for you to wash up before dinner, okay? Just you guys?" Jilly said gently as she freed a hand to pat the boy's thin shoulder. "Gracie can wash up here at the sink, and then we'll all eat. Go ahead, Nicholas," she said, rubbing the bony point of his small, vulnerable shoulder. "It's okay."

Kids could break your heart. And these two were both wounded little birds in their own way. She knew Gracie's wounds, and sensed that Nicholas carried his own burdens of memory and pain.

"I want my mommy," he said in a voice that quivered with echoes of Gracie's sobs. "And my Jake."

"You won't feel so bad with a little—" she sought a word that would lift his head "—with a little grub under your belt, Nicholas."

"Maybe." He turned his head toward her and the downward curve of his mouth trembled. His blue eyes, so like his mother's, were woeful under spiky-wet eyelashes.

"I know that's what Hank would suggest." Jilly shifted Gracie's weight to her other hip as the little girl turned her head to watch Nicholas. Jilly didn't know why she was using Hank as her parental guru, Hank with no children and no apparent interest in a relationship outside the long-burning flame for his sister-in-law, but he was the only other adult within reach. "Hank would say working guys needed hot chow." Chow? Was that a cowboy kind of word? She hoped so.

"But I want to go *home!*" Nicholas insisted.

"All right. If you still feel that way after dinner, we'll call Sarah and Jake to come get you. Or you can call them. How's that? You know how to use the phone, right?"

Nicholas nodded slowly. "I can call on the phone. I know my number, and Mommy wrote the number for me." He stood up, pushing the chair back under the table with both hands. He nodded again, his solemn face lighting up. "I'll call them. They'll want to hear from me."

"And in the meantime, you and Gracie can talk at dinner, all right?"

"All right." Silent for a moment as he wrinkled his forehead, clearly weighing the importance of what he was going to do, he finally nodded his head once more before trudging off down the hallway. "I'll surprise them."

Turning to watch him, Jilly tightened her arms around her still-quiet daughter. Seconds later, she heard the boy's tentative knock on the bathroom door, his questioning treble and then the low tones of Hank's voice responding. The door opened. A muscular, soapy arm held the door as Nicholas ducked through it. Soap dotted the hallway as the arm pulled the door shut.

"I don't want Nickels to go home," Gracie whispered into Jilly's ear. "Make him stay, Mommy."

Jilly wished she could hear Hank's conversation with the half-pint male.

Looking at the white soap spots, she felt that traitorous slide of heat curling through her as an image of a soap-lathered, sleek-skinned adult male flashed in her brain.

Jilly shut her eyes.

Oh, Callie had no idea, none at all, how impossible Hank Tyler would be to ignore.

She swallowed.

Chapter Five

"**I** thought you said you weren't going to cook?" Hank's hand hovered near the rim of the platter piled with chicken.

"I said that, yes." Jilly tipped her head dismissively in his general direction, indicating her lack of interest in pursuing the issue.

"But you did?"

"Obviously." She waggled the platter at him.

"Why?"

"It's Sunday."

"Yeah. So?"

"Because." She didn't see any need to reveal what now struck her as a kind of small-minded pettiness in trying to compete with him. Still, she hadn't been entirely motivated by competition. She had wanted to pay a kind of debt, but his questions were making her ill at ease. They were making her examine her actions more closely than she wanted to. She thrust the platter at him. "Come on, Hatty. Eat. The food's getting cold."

"Hatty? Getting touchy, are we? A wee bit defensive?"
He took the platter, speared three pieces of crisply brown
chicken. "And *because* isn't an answer, you know, princess."

"I changed my mind. I cooked." That should end it. Jilly
wanted him to move on to a different subject. Mostly,
though, she wanted to escape his narrowed, focused gaze
that glimmered with a shade too much curiosity. "Anyway, what difference does it make?"

"Mostly because," he replied, his voice infinitely pa-
tient, "you made it real clear, princess, that you weren't
going to be chief cook and bottle washer while you were
here." Putting the platter down, he held his hands palms up
in a universal sign of surrender. "Not that I blame you."
He lifted an eyebrow. "So what I'm strangely curious about
is why you changed your mind."

Pushed into a corner, Jilly glared at him. "Exactly what
I said. You cooked that enormous breakfast for the kids. I
owed you. That's all."

"Mommy—"

Nicholas's gaze flew to hers. "But—"

"You didn't need to go to all this trouble because you
thought—" He paused, ran his palm over the linen cloth,
shot a glance at Nicholas and Gracie, who sank back into
their chairs as he spoke. "Anyway, I was hungry. They
were, too. We all needed food. You were tired. They
weren't. No sense in disturbing you. Except they did."
Hank plopped a spoonful of mashed potatoes on Gracie's
plate, then on Nicholas's. "There you go, ranch hands. Fill
up. You both worked hard." Thumping the serving spoon
free of mashed potatoes, he leaned forward for the gravy
bowl, and his eyes met hers.

Unreadable, his expression was as bland as egg custard.
But for a crazy second, Jilly thought he looked sheepish.
And that made no sense at all.

They were seated at the dining room table, Gracie and
Nicholas facing each other on opposite sides of the long

rectangle, she and Hank staring at each other down the length of linen and age-worn silverware as he half rose from his seat to reach for the tureen. "Pass the gravy?"

Studying him closely, Jilly handed him the creamy white saucer and bowl. As he took it, the side of his hand brushed along her palm. She jerked her hand back, and silky brown gravy dotted the table. Quickly looking away from him, her hand imprinted with that skimming touch, she dipped her napkin in her water glass and dabbed at the spots.

Nicholas's treble broke the silence. "But, Hank, we—"

The ladle clinked against the bowl. "Nicholas?" A second clink. Gracie fidgeted, started to speak, then stopped. Nicholas's chair scraped on the floor.

Looking at the three of them, Jilly saw their glances pass back and forth. But nobody spoke. Lifting spoons and forks industriously, they absorbed themselves in the meal.

She'd found a heavy linen tablecloth, the white threads mellowed with age into a buttery cream color. She'd used the beautiful cloth without a qualm. The impulse to set a *House Beautiful* Sunday table had come straight out of her need to show Hank Tyler.

Show him what? How wrong he was about her? Even though she didn't care what he thought? Setting the table with satisfaction, she'd practically measured the distances between plates and silverware with a ruler. Not entirely consumed with what had become a contest for her, though, she'd used plastic cups and plates from the kitchen cupboard for Gracie and Nicholas.

Watching them, she couldn't escape the feeling that something was up. But whatever was going on couldn't have anything to do with the dinner. She stirred the well of mashed potatoes and gravy on her plate with satisfaction. Nobody could fault this meal. The fried chicken and milk gravy were perfect.

Even Larry would have approved. Except that he never ate anything fried. Or slathered with gravy. Unless it came with a French label.

He'd even bought her a complete set of epicurean cook-books and paid for several courses in the preparation of French cuisine. And Italian. And Thai.

She'd enjoyed making cappelletti and pastas from scratch, blanching broccoli and making vegetarian lasagnas. Heck, with cholesterol, low-fat no-fat and beta carotenes mentioned in the news every day, she preferred broiled, baked and steamed on a regular basis herself. She knew she would have cooked in much the same way, even without Larry's guiding hand.

But if she sometimes thought his food preferences had more to do with the fad of the moment than with health or pleasure, she kept her impressions to herself.

Yet sometimes she'd felt as if she was being graded in their own kitchen, in their bedroom—

Jilly pushed the troubling memories away in much the same way Gracie was energetically shoving the pile of almonds she'd culled from her green beans off to the side of her plate. She and Nicholas were eating the green beans, though, without audible protesting.

"Ready for dessert?" She didn't know Nicholas, but she knew her daughter. "Chocolate cake. Homemade. As a thank-you to the three of you for letting me sleep in. For cooking breakfast and cleaning up. You did a great job." Jilly refrained from looking at Hank, but she caught Gracie's openmouthed glance in his direction.

Wondering why the two children kept staring at Hank, Jilly stood up to get the cake from the sideboard. She would find out eventually. Gracie couldn't keep a secret.

"Hank! Tell Mommy—" Gracie hadn't learned that a whisper required a relatively lower volume.

"Cake looks good." Hank's voice sounded strangled. "You baked it from scratch, huh?"

Suspicious, Jilly placed the cake plate carefully on the table. "Yes. That's what I said."

"Really looks good. Took a while, did it? Mixing? Stirring? All that?"

"Yes." Taking three dessert plates, Jilly slowly sliced through the rich chocolate frosting, down through the moist cake. "A lot of stirring. And mixing." She paused, the knife held upright, its silver blade coated with frosting and crumbs. And then, looking at Gracie's busting-to-tell face, Jilly knew exactly what had happened. A dark brown, glossy crumb landed on the tablecloth as she pointed the knife at Hank. "You sneak."

"Shoot." He grimaced. "Reckon you could lower your knife, sugar? For a minute?"

"I don't think so." Jilly tapped the cake knife menacingly against the plate she held out to him. "What a low-down, *awful* man you are, Hank Tyler. You let me think—" She sputtered to a halt, regrouped as she handed Gracie and Nicholas their plates. "No wonder the kitchen was so clean. You didn't even boil water in there this morning, much less cook hash browns. And eggs. Or grits!"

"You guessed, huh?" Hank was still staying out of her knife range, Jilly noticed, as he used the potato spoon to urge the cake closer.

"But we did have grits and ham and all that, Mommy," Gracie reassured Jilly through a mouth filled with cake. "Really. And we took our trays up to the trash afterward. Hank made us."

"Did he?" With her free hand, Jilly wiped her daughter's mouth with a napkin. "And where did Hank take you to eat, sweetie?"

"Hank took them to the Cluck and Oink." He settled the dessert plate in front of him.

"You double-dealing lying fiend." Placing the knife carefully down on the cake plate, Jilly was terribly tempted to toss the whole cake at him. In her vexation, the creamy brown dessert cake struck her as a lethal weapon. "Hanging's too good for you."

"Probably." He licked his finger free of the frosting he'd stolen while her attention was on his perfidy. "Awfully good cake," he said.

Eyes wide and fascinated above frosting-smeared mouths, Gracie and Nicholas were silent.

"The Cluck and Oink?" Groaning, Jilly sank into her chair and covered her eyes. "You're kidding? Right? That has to be a joke."

"Nope. Sorry, sugar, but it's the redneck version of Mickey Dee."

Jilly surveyed the bowls, the plates, the fried chicken, the linen.

And the cake.

The damned cake that had taken the biggest part of the morning because the first one had fallen apart when she'd taken it out of the cake pans. "I've been cooking since six-thirty this morning because I thought you'd fixed all that *stuff* for breakfast. And cleaned up! I thought you'd cleaned up that—that *mess!*" Jilly looked again at the table crowded with food and dirty dishes, thought with dismay about the still-unscrubbed pots in the kitchen. "And I felt guilty."

Loaded with icing and cake, his fork hesitated in front of his mouth as Hank shot her a quick, assessing look that she didn't understand. "Even if I had cooked all that food and cleaned up, why should *you* feel guilty? That's a heavy load to carry. And, besides, feeling guilty wastes a lot of energy, princess."

"What I wasted was this whole morning, wasted it trying to show you— I'm a fool," Jilly said. She cleared her throat. "An idiot. A nincompoop."

"I never said I cooked breakfast, princess." His voice was low, too gentle, and her eyes prickled with sudden tears.

"No. You didn't." She stared out the window until she could bring the unexpected teariness under control. She didn't understand this confusing emotion that churned up her insides and tightened her throat, but his offhand comment had bumped some heretofore unknown pain.

"And I didn't ask you to spend all morning in the kitchen."

Again that gentleness in his voice undermined her control, and she couldn't grasp why it seemed so threatening.

"True." Jilly knew exactly why she'd changed her mind. "It was my decision. My choice."

He leaned back in his chair, his arms stretched overhead. Fixed on her, his gaze was intense, and Jilly stirred, having the impression they were no longer talking about the dinner she'd cooked. "Nobody was making a fuss over meals. Except you, princess," he added gently, never taking his eyes away from hers. "So what's the big deal?"

Thinking of the wasted hours, the effort, the cleaning still to be done, Jilly wanted to tell him what the "big deal" was, but she couldn't.

Because cooking wasn't the issue. Faced with his questions, she realized that something besides paying debts and competing had driven her. She was absolutely certain that she didn't want to examine any closer the motivations that had led her into kitchen mania, so she simply shrugged. "You're right. No big deal. It had nothing to do with you."

"No?" He leaned farther away from her, and the sense of threat should have been reduced. It wasn't. "Who with, then?"

Sunlight streamed in through the wide, long windows, splashed the creamy old tablecloth with yellow. Nicholas's glass rattled against the edge of his plastic plate.

Her thumb resting on the smooth, cool handle of the knife, Jilly stared at Hank, uneasy with the thoughts slithering under the surface of her consciousness. "I was... tired. I overreacted."

"Did you? You don't seem like a woman who loses her temper. Like a woman who overreacts." Hank shook his head, and with each slow movement of his sun-bright hair,

Jilly felt tension wind tighter and tighter inside her. "Why did you feel so guilty about my feeding the kids?"

The sunshine burned along her arm, and caught in that moment that vibrated with other, unwanted questions, Jilly was silent.

"Why, princess?"

"I don't know, but I do know that if you call me princess one more time, so help me, I won't be responsible." Retreating into the immediacy of attending to her daughter's needs, Jilly handed Gracie a napkin and gestured for her to wipe her mouth.

"And you with that big old knife so close to hand." He faked a shudder, and Gracie giggled. "Well, I reckon a smart man would walk right carefully around you. In case you overreacted, or something."

Nicholas snickered and then covered his mouth with both hands, his bright blue eyes wide above his clasped fingers.

And then, his gaze never leaving hers, Hank rested his elbows on the table and leaned closer, leaving Jilly grateful they were at opposite ends of the old piece of furniture.

As he leaned forward, a different kind of tension vibrated between them, sputtering and popping like water drops on a hot skillet as he said, "Best cake I ever had, *Jilly*. And I was hungry."

Her stomach quivered, but, like Hank, she stuck her finger into the frosting, licked it off. "It is good, isn't it?"

"Better than my mama's." His eyes sparkled.

"Really?" Jilly didn't trust the man an inch, not when his eyes held that glint.

"Easy. Hers were all store-bought."

"I see."

"She didn't like to cook. Except for special occasions," he said, smiling.

Blinding her, his smile was a miracle of sweetness. Its warmth flooded her, its heat suffused her, and Jilly blinked against it, felt it moving through her like warm cocoa, soothing her turmoil.

"Lumpy potatoes went down as fast at our house as perfectly whipped ones. Tasted as good," he continued. "And Mama never felt guilty about her lumpy potatoes or overcooked spaghetti. She said if we wanted perfection, we could do it ourselves. She used to laugh as hard as we did when the meals came out looking, well, 'right peculiar' is what she called them." He laughed, and the white lines around his green-blue eyes radiated in his tanned skin.

"Peculiar?"

"Yep." He grinned. "Spam with pineapple slices on top of canned baked beans was fancy cooking in this house when I was growing up."

Jilly smiled. "I suppose it could be...tasty."

"We liked it. But have you ever had tacos made with spinach? Mama swore up and down it was nothing more than exceptionally dark lettuce. Too much rain. Or too little."

"Healthful, at least." She picked up her dessert plate, put it back down. The spinach tacos story would have been food for laughter for years, a different kind of nourishing.

"Sure. But we never knew for certain whether Mama knew the difference or not. Buck swore she did. T.J. said she didn't. Daddy said it didn't matter."

"Spinch tacos?" Nicholas wrinkled up his face at Gracie. "I like tacos. I don't like spinch. Never. Not even on tacos I wouldn't."

"I like it," Gracie said staunchly. "With bread stuff on it."

Sighing, Jilly picked up the plate, stacked Gracie's and Nicholas's on top of hers. "You had fun, didn't you?"

He slid the potato bowl back and forth, waiting a beat before he said, "Why don't you want me to call you princess, Jilly? Nothing but a nickname. Suits you, you know." He was serious now, changing the rhythm of their conversation and throwing her off balance.

"That was Larry's special name for me."

"I see." He shifted, and Jilly heard the scrape of his chair legs against the wooden floor. "Your husband. Gracie's father."

"Yes."

"And he died."

Placing her palms flat on the table, Jilly was aware only of the texture of the linen cloth, the intensity of Hank's gaze. He was so close suddenly, his wide shoulders filling her view. "Yes, Hank. He died. Seven months ago. In an accident. And he was the most wonderful husband in the world. No one could have been kinder or gentler or more hardworking—or more thoughtful. Everything he did, he did for me. For Gracie. He was—"

"A prince?" Hank's slightly mocking smile curved the ends of his mouth.

"Yes. He was." That smile with its skepticism lit a spark of anger in Jilly and made her rush into speech. "*Everybody* knew how wonderful he was, what a terrific husband and father. All our friends said so."

"How nice," Hank drawled, his eyes shadowed now by one of his wide hands. "A paragon. A saint among men."

Her voice went raspy with anger and heat. If there had been gentleness in his voice, it would have been easier, but she heard doubt, or thought she did, and she needed to make him see, needed to make him believe what a special man Larry had been. She needed to remind herself, too, after these last weeks. "He was. Absolutely. And every time you call me princess, I think of him. And I can't stand it."

"Can't stand what, sugar? Me calling you by his pet name? Or thinking of him? I'm interested. What exactly is it you can't stand?"

"Both." She looked down at the table where her fingers had wadded the cloth into lumps under the pressure of her grip. Looking away from Hank, she said, "And it's not your concern. Curiosity doesn't always require satisfaction."

"No," he said, and his next words came slowly, "it doesn't. And you're right. It's not my concern."

"Okay, then." She took a deep breath, feeling as if she'd walked over a shaking forest bridge. "Okay."

"Right. Okay." He smiled, and she felt the impact right down to her toes and found her breath catching in her throat. "Changing the subject, this was a terrific dinner, Jilly." He pushed his chair back from the table and stood up. "But I'm real sorry you felt you had to fix all this." He waved his hand at the table. "Shoot, sugar, paper napkins and plastic would have been good enough."

"But it's Sunday," Jilly protested, her voice dying away in the silence between them as he studied her.

Finally, picking up plates and glasses, he said, "And that was important to you, wasn't it?"

She nodded, her throat closing on her.

"I know you worked hard, Jilly. And it *was* the best meal I've had in a long time. So thank you. For taking the time to do this for me. For us."

Again her eyes prickled with tears.

Suddenly she realized how much she'd missed the country cooking of her childhood, the greens simmered all Sunday morning in "pot likker," as her grandmother used to call the broth flavored with salt pork, the platters piled high with fried chicken, and bowls of rice pudding, the flavor of which Jilly had never been able to duplicate, but which she suspected had come strongly seasoned with love.

Perhaps something of that instinct had also been working deep inside her, a yearning for the past, for simpler ways, for a time rendered perfect by memory. Jilly sighed. So many years had passed since those days. So much had happened. So many things she couldn't change.

Sunlight burnished the faint shadows along Hank's jaw and turned his light brown hair gold as he knuckled Nicholas's head and made the boy chortle. "Grab a bowl, squirt, and make a beeline for the kitchen. Them what eats, cleans."

Nicholas popped out of his chair and grabbed bowls and glasses with cheerful abandon, Gracie following right on his heels, making buzzing sounds.

Leading his half-pint troops toward the kitchen, Hank strolled toward the dining room arch, his long legs moving like well-oiled pistons.

"Come on, Nickels, me and you can dry knives and forks." Restored by food to equanimity, Gracie smiled sweetly at the boy as the two trailed Hank out the room.

Gracie and Nicholas were friends again.

"See you, prin—sugar," Hank drawled from the kitchen. "Don't come into the kitchen. Elves are at work in here. Shut your eyes and who knows what will happen."

"Disaster?" Stifling her chuckle, Jilly made her tone as sweet as pecan pie.

Drat the man. He'd run her through more emotions in the last twenty-four hours than she'd felt in months.

Hank's family hadn't had perfect dinners. They'd had lumpy potatoes and love.

Looking at the sunshine filling the dining room, glowing on the tablecloth and silver and gilding the pine planks of the floor, Jilly had the sense of something rare and precious living in the house. She sensed that the love that seeped into every object, every room of the house, was the sun that warmed Hank Tyler and gave him strength to push back the shadows, gave him the strength of character to sacrifice himself for love of his brother.

His easygoing ways could make a careless person underestimate him.

Underneath his mellow, go-with-the-flow nonchalance were grit and steel.

Grit enough to recognize the truth of his feelings.

Steel enough not to act on them.

Head bowed, shoulders slumped, Jilly pleated the napkin between her fingers. It slipped back and forth between her fingers as she listened to the sounds of dishes and running water.

Hank was right. Guilt had a weight beyond measuring. She rubbed the back of her neck. Why hadn't she recognized that guilt was part of the equation?

Splashes came from the kitchen. "All right, guys. No soap on the head honcho. That's mutiny." A big wet splash. Drips. "There, now y'all are decorated, too."

A deep rumble and squeals of laughter distracted her from her unwelcome realization. Throwing down the napkin, she stood up. She knew it wasn't guilt that drew her to the kitchen crew. No, what drew her to the doorway was the sound of her daughter's laughter.

And loneliness.

A loneliness so deep inside she couldn't remember when it hadn't been there, at the core of her being.

She wanted to be with noise and teasing and—

Gathering up the remaining plates, she took a deep breath.

What drew her out of the dining room was the satin-smooth drawl of Hank Tyler.

With her hands filled, she halted outside the kitchen, staring inside, suddenly unsure of herself. All three were covered with soapsuds that shone rainbow colors in the light. Doubled over with laughter, they looked at her, the same surprised expression on each face. They were a team, *together* in some indefinable way.

There was no place for her in their closed circle of silliness.

She should have stayed in the dining room or gone for a walk. She should have done anything else but intrude, because now she felt like a gawky teenager with no place to sit in the high school lunchroom.

The outsider.

Swatting soapsuds out of his eyes, Hank turned to the doorway.

He'd known she was there. The skin along the back of his neck had tightened. Maybe it was the subliminal scent of her. Maybe nothing more than the subconsciously heard sound of her steps, light though they were.

But he'd known.

"I thought you could use another pair of hands." She shifted, lifted one shoulder, and the rippling silver shine of her blouse curved in and tightened, flattening the softness of her breasts.

His attention caught by the pull of fabric between waist and breast, Hank felt as if one of his brothers had landed a hard, straight punch right to his middle and left him unable to breathe, unable to speak. Staring at Jilly as she stood indecisively at the doorway, he felt his body responding.

Subconscious, subliminal or plain old primitive male hormones, whatever it was, yeah, his instincts recognized something. Like a private in the army, his body was standing alert and at attention. Ready, willing and able.

In fact, far more willing than was comfortable for a man in old, too-tight jeans. Shoot, and women thought they were at a disadvantage.

"So, what do you think, guys?" Half turning to the sink, Hank shoved his hands into his side pockets. Giving nature a chance to calm down, he slouched, one hip against the sink as he focused on multiplication tables and vectors and capitals of the fifty states. "Do we need help?"

"Yep," said Nicholas.

"Nope," said Gracie. "We got it under control. Me and Hank do."

Lifting one hand, Jilly brushed back her hair. Like polished oak, the dark brown strands slipped through her fingers. With her movement, delicate gray lace peeked out of the unbuttoned neck of her shirt, vanished as she lowered her arm.

"I get the tiebreaker vote, huh?" He was up to Kentucky and about to break out in a sweat. Hell, what *was* the damned capital of the state? Louisville? Frankfort? Yeah,

Frankfort. "Sheesh. Decisions, decisions. All this pressure, guys."

The narrow metal belt around her waist kept his gaze fixed on the rise and fall of her breasts, made him notice the increasingly shallow breaths she took.

And he didn't want to notice. Didn't want to see how the gray slacks shaped the slopes of her hips. Didn't want to think about the way his palms would fit, like so, over those curves. His fingers curved into his palms.

Nine times thirteen was . . . hell, what was it?

Not moving, he watched the fragile blue vein that pulsed at the side of her neck, the slow beating only a flutter under her skin.

Silver coils dangled from her earlobes, brushed against the side of her cheek, slid back into the mink richness of her hair and then as she bent her head, winked forward once again, cool silver against the peony pink of her cheeks.

His fingertips tingled.

His whole body buzzed.

Eight times eight is sixty-four. Washington. Seattle.

Hank turned his head and yanked his hands out of his pockets. Flipping on the faucet, he rinsed off a plate. With his back to her, he said, "Well, sugar, I figured you'd done the hard work, cooking and all, and you deserved to kick back if you wanted to."

"Kicking back isn't my style."

"No?"

In the window reflection to the side of the kitchen, he watched her fingers tighten around the plates she held in her hands. She shook her head and her heavy hair swung in one scythe-shaped curve against her neck. "Makes me nervous."

"Yeah?"

"Yeah. Very nervous." There wasn't even a hint of a smile in the demurely tucked-in corners of her mouth, but he was learning, and he recognized the teasing in the way she imitated his drawled question.

"Wouldn't want to make you all distraught and nervous, sugar, so what the heck. Come on in, we'll find something for you to do."

"I don't want to be in the way." In the reflection, he watched her take a baby-size step forward, and he sensed another emotion behind her teasing response.

"You won't be. It's a big kitchen." He shut his eyes, opened them to stare at the sink with its bowls and plates.

Not even looking at her, he could *see* her. Could see those deep blue eyes with their uneasy wariness. And anxiety. Her caution intrigued him. Her anxiety pulled at him, made him want to shine a light in the dark corners of her world so that she wouldn't be frightened.

And that urge surprised the hell out of him. He hadn't felt this kind of protective urge toward a woman since—

Clearing her throat, she took a step back, away from the kitchen. "Well, perhaps I'll— Or I could—"

"Yeah? Could what?" He turned around, faced her.

"I could take a walk." She sighed, and he didn't think she realized she'd done so. "I'm awfully full. A walk would be nice. After a big meal like that. I'm not used to heavy meals." She sighed again.

The princess had things on her mind. Subjects she had no intention of discussing, that was clear. He was becoming increasingly more interested in ferreting out those secrets that hovered in the darkness of her eyes, in the tension around her mouth.

"Walks are good," he agreed.

"Hmm."

"More fun with company."

"Yes, that's true," she said, taking another step into the kitchen and looking at him with that unconscious awareness, that feminine recognition that called to him in spite of himself. She wouldn't like knowing how wide and misty-blue her eyes went when she looked at him, wouldn't like knowing how soft her mouth became.

"We could go for a walk later. All of us. In the meantime, come on in and join the party."

"Sure?" The rosy fullness of her mouth shaped the word.

"Plenty of cleaning up left. Step right up." Not looking at her, he pointed toward the stack of plates with food still clinging to them.

"You put these dishes in the machine?" she asked.

"Yep." He gave Gracie a bowl. "Careful, sugar dumpling."

"But they're so old. Shouldn't we wash them by hand? They must be valuable."

"They're only dishes, Jilly."

"But the machine will ruin them."

"Maybe sometime, but our folks always acted on the belief that you used whatever you had. The Tylers didn't set up altars to cars and dishes. They could be replaced. Objects were meant to be used, enjoyed. So don't worry about the dishes. Help if you want to." He wanted her to stay. But he wouldn't ask her to. Water splashed against his chest as he tipped a plate at the wrong angle.

Hesitating once more, touching a bowl with the tip of her finger, she shrugged. "If it's okay, I'd like to stay." She picked up a plate and scraped it. "But I don't want to be a bother." Bits of chicken and bones landed on top of the food scraps already in the plastic bag intended for the hogs.

"You won't be." He heard the scrape of her fork against the china, the plop of food into the bag. He would swear he could hear the scrape of that gray lace against her skin as she moved. "Don't worry about it, sugar."

A bother? In the way? Hell, yes, he was bothered. And the worst of it was that he could tell he *bothered* her, just a speck. For a man, that was a powerful lure. That combination of feminine wariness and vulnerability stirred all kinds of right primitive instincts.

He handed a rinsed plate to Gracie, who proceeded to show Nicholas "zactly how you gotta stack it." Apparently intent on preserving their restored friendship, Nicholas did as he was told.

Amused by Gracie's earnest perfectionism, Hank grinned.

Glancing at Jilly, he wondered at the frown that drew her eyebrows together, even though she didn't say anything to her daughter. "Don't worry. They're fine," he said in an undertone. "They're bonded by food and soapsuds."

"Perhaps." She glanced toward her daughter once more but didn't elaborate. She handed Hank the scraped bowls and the last plate. "I hope so. Gracie's—" Jilly stopped.

"He taught her something this morning. Now it's her turn." Hank figured that, given time, the kids would find their own ways of equalizing their friendship.

"I suppose. Anything else to scrape?"

Intending to add that he and T.J. and Buck had had their share of squabbles and make-ups, Hank leaned toward her. As he did, she turned to look at the counter and stove. One smooth bit of hair lifted with her turn and whispered past the edge of his mouth.

Not thinking, he reached out to capture the gleaming strand. Lifting it to his mouth, inhaling the sweetness of its scent, he wanted to wrap his fist into the glossy texture of her hair and pull her face to his, hard. He had enough good sense not to, but he must have tugged because she twisted her head abruptly and her mouth brushed the length of his finger. With the strand of hair still wrapped around his finger, Hank touched the tip of his finger to the center of her bottom lip, pressing its supple warmth, and the ends of the strand of hair traced the deep curve.

She shivered and grew very still, her pupils going a lovely, lovely blue that made him think about those final seconds of loving and the instant before everything went over the edge. He reckoned any man would count himself lucky to see Gillian Elliott's eyes go muzzy-blue and filled with him in those moments.

"An accident," she whispered, not looking away.

"You know what Freud said." Releasing the silk ribbon of her hair, Hank lowered his hand, his arm, slowly, reluctantly. Unwanted, unexpected, a thought flashed in his head. Both Jake and Jilly had said Larry Elliott's death was the result of an accident. "He said there are no accidents."

"This was." She reached blindly for the closest plate, scraping it with shaking hands. "Believe me, *this* was an accident." She extended the plate to him, her arm, hand, fingers, carefully out of accidental touching range. Her face was troubled as she looked straight at him. "Hank, don't play these games with me, please. I thought we settled this last night." Her hands were white against the cream tone of the china plate she held tightly in front of her. "You're way out of my league. I'm not a casual person. Flirting and making casual contact come as easily to you as breathing, but I don't know the rules for games like these anymore. It's been too long, and I was never any good at them to begin with."

Hank took the piece of china before her shaking fingers let it clatter against the edge of the sink and break. "Whatever you say, sugar."

"No more games?"

"No more games," he agreed. But that moment when he'd touched her hadn't been part of a male-female game. That moment had disturbed him with its *realness*.

"Good." Her voice was breathy. "We'll all be more comfortable that way."

"Think so?"

"Oh, yes." She gave him a dazzling smile as she reached for the last bowl. "Definitely."

Not likely was his considered opinion, but he'd been wrong at least once or twice in thirty-three years.

Comfortable wasn't how the princess made him feel. Aroused, every nerve in his body twanging like a guitar string, sounding to an ancient need. Those reactions he understood.

Not comfortable at all, but familiar.

With the scent of her all around him and the feel of her mouth still lingering on his hand, he couldn't help wondering if Larry the Paragon had been all that terrific.

She was sweet, funny and edgy underneath her coolly elegant exterior. Way too edgy.

The princess was distressed about something. Even though she thought she hid it, the signs were there in those shadows, in the way she looked at her daughter sometimes, and, most of all, in the tension that strung her as tightly as a piano wire.

He wondered if Saint Larry the Terrific had put the shadows in her eyes. A flash of animosity speared through him.

Grief? Was that what he saw in her eyes? Or something else?

Not moving, stunned by her smile, abruptly he decided he was going to find out.

Lawrence Elliott might have been a prince, but Hank didn't think so.

No matter how many polite bricks she stacked into the wall around her, thinking she could keep everyone on the other side of her castle walls, he was of a mind to charge right through.

But the hell of it was that he couldn't figure out why he was so determined to break down all those carefully mortared fortifications. That part confused him, and he couldn't sort it out.

He knew he liked teasing her, stirring her up until her skin pinkened with annoyance, liked seeing her anger melt that cool serenity into genuine emotions. Liked shaking her out of her emotional passivity.

He liked seeing her come alive, as if she were waking up after a long, long sleep. Liked seeing her the way she was now, head tilted as she looked up at him, her eyes soft, her mouth half curved in the last traces of her smile.

If he decided he was going to call her princess, he would.

The sudden aggression surprised him. He didn't like it. It unsettled him, made him testy. He wasn't used to those feelings.

Irritated with himself, Hank turned off the faucet with a violence that left his fist clenched.

Saint Larry be damned.

Chapter Six

"So what about that walk?" The adrenaline sparking crankily along his nerve endings needed an outlet. "Anybody want to join me?" Hank leaned against the spotless, empty sink and crossed his arms as he watched Jilly drape the towel across the metal rod.

She'd turned back the cuffs on her long-sleeved blouse and a narrow-banded gold watch rode loosely over the small bones of one wrist. Diamonds framed the watch face and sparkled against black numerals. It was a frivolous, expensive watch, a watch fit for a princess who wouldn't be sticking her hands in sudsy hot water all the time. He didn't like that dainty little plaything.

"I'm ready for fresh air. Who's coming?" He looked down at the light weight resting against him. In a one-legged stork stance, Nicholas had propped himself casually against Hank's leg. He thumped the boy gently on the head. "How about you guys?"

"Yeah." Nicholas reached down and scratched his ankle.

"I want to go see the horses again," Gracie said, tilting her round face with its undefined cheekbones up to him. Her tangle of brown hair flopped into her eyes. "Pretty please?" she added, batting her thick, stubby eyelashes at him. Her smile was a mixture of the sweetness of her mother's and her own determined nature. "It would be *very* delightful."

Amused by her steamroller combination of engaging forthrightness and persistence, he managed not to grin back at her. "Yes, I can see that it would be—delightful. Tell you what, Miss Gracie, I have to do some minor repair on a horse's hoof. How would you and Nicholas like to help out?"

"Oh, yes! Thank you very, very much," she said, patting his hand and whirling to Nicholas. "Come on, Nickels! You can show me what to do this time, and I will listen very carefully, all right?"

"Yeah, I guess."

"Wait on the porch or in the front yard," Jilly called to their retreating backs as the screen door to the kitchen slammed behind them.

"Yes, ma'am," Gracie said from the other side of the screen door.

"And, Gracie, don't go out of sight."

"We won't." Skidding to a halt, Gracie turned to press her face against the screen. "And I will not let Nickels get into any trouble while we are waiting. I promise I will be responsible. You do not have to worry about me and Nickels. Bye!"

And she was gone, running to catch up with Nicholas, whose boots thumped in a punka-punka rhythm against the boards of the porch as he raced toward the front swing.

"I wish I could bottle up their energy and take a teaspoonful every hour or so." Jilly unrolled her cuffs and fastened them at her wrists. "Gracie has two speeds. Full ahead and stop. But she's usually not so—"

"So?"

Jilly wrinkled her nose. "Volatile. Emotional."

In eight or nine years, Hank figured Gracie would be a force to be reckoned with. The princess would have her hands full. He had a sneaking suspicion that Saint Larry hadn't been much help in keeping the baby autocrat on the straight and narrow. Bright and spunky, Gracie was no sit-com saccharine cutie. That she wasn't a brat was a kind of miracle. Or maybe the result of a behind-the-scenes strength he hadn't seen in the princess. "I wouldn't call her volatile."

"No?" A fleeting smile moved across her face. "What then? And keep in mind that mothers are notoriously ferocious in defending their young."

Hank checked around the sink and counter. "No knives in sight. Reckon I'm safe?"

"Perhaps." Her smile widened, softened the strain around her mouth.

"I don't know diddly about baby girls, and maybe things are a whole lot different, but if Gracie were a boy, Jilly, no one would think twice about her—"

"Her bossiness?"

"Uh, that. Yeah. She's bossy." He jammed his hands into his back pockets so that he wouldn't give in to the temptation to smooth that furrow between the wings of her silky eyebrows. "If she were a boy, you'd call it leadership, you know. Or organization."

"Think so?"

"Lord, if you'd seen me and my brothers, you'd know what I mean. Gracie's a tough little cookie, Jilly. She's strong. She's allowed to be as bossy as a boy, I think. She's real clear about what she wants, and she's not afraid to go after it. Those are great qualities. We admire them in adults, don't we? Why shouldn't Gracie be admired for her strength? Her energy?"

"I don't want her running over people in her hurry to reach whatever she's decided she wants." Jilly ran her fingers through her hair, fluffing it out, and the strands fell smoothly in place, sending him a faint drift of her forest-clean fragrance.

He inhaled the scent, took it deep inside him before he realized what he'd done. Exhaling slowly, he felt a curious sense of loss. "Think she'd do that? Run over people?"

"Actually, these days, I'm not sure what she'll do next." Wrapping her arms around herself, Jilly looked out the window as the kids ran pell-mell past it, Gracie's short legs pumping in a blur of speed. "And I worry that she's too aggressive, that she's become too demanding, too—"

She walked over to the window, pressed her forehead to it. "Anyway, I worry." Backlit by the sun flooding in through the window, Jilly's figure was in silhouette, a silky harmony of fragile curves.

"She doesn't seem especially aggressive to me, Jilly." Hank strolled over and stood behind her, watching the racing children with her. "But what do I know? Hell, I grew up with two older brothers who thought they were being gentle with me if they kept the horses and cattle from tromping on my skull."

A smile touched Jilly's lips as she glanced up at him. "Brotherly love. I'm impressed."

"Me, too." Remembering the tomfoolery that had gotten out of control once in a while, making the three swear on a stack of Bibles never to let the folks know, Hank chuckled. "Hell, they could have fed me to the pigs in a moment of inspiration. Listen, sugar, Gracie's only a kid. Shoot, she reminds me a lot of Sarah Jane when she would come to the ranch for a visit. And Callie, too, when she first started dating T.J." Thinking of the seventeen-year-old Callie who'd captivated him with her cheerful coltishness and determination to do the right thing, Hank touched the window.

Being in the house again brought all the memories and feelings rushing back. So many years. Sometimes he felt like a car stranded on the highway, everybody else whizzing on by, leaving him behind. He sighed.

Jilly stepped to the side, away from him. "But Gracie used to be so quiet. Sweeter, I think. Not so—" Clearly avoiding his gaze, she rested her forehead against the window. "I don't know. It's confusing sometimes. All these changes." As she inclined her head, her hair parted at the back of her neck, sweeping forward to reveal that sweet spot at the base of her scalp where pale skin showed and brown tendrils curled against the soft gray cotton collar of her blouse.

One tendril lay trapped under the edge of the collar, and as lightly as he would touch a baby's skin, so lightly that Jilly would never know, he lifted the strand free. Vanishing in the mass of sleek brown, it slid under the weight of the rest of her hair.

She stirred restlessly, rubbed her arms as if chilled.

And an aching need slashed through him, leaving him breathless, breathless like a thief listening for the shrieking of a burglar alarm. "She's changed?" His words were hoarse.

"She's been in tears twice now in two days, and that's not like her. She used to be so even-tempered. For a five-year-old." Jilly laid her left hand against the glass. Her slim palm and narrow fingers cupped the distant figures of the children. Her ring, too large for the delicate shape of her hands, caught his attention as it glittered maliciously in the kitchen lights.

Suddenly, irritability tensed his muscles, and he rolled his shoulders. Maybe for reasons of her own, the princess needed Gracie to be the sitcom cutie he thought she wasn't. "I'd expect a five-year-old whose dad died a few months ago to be off stride. Confused. A whole lot crankier than Gracie seems. She must miss her dad." He wondered how much Gracie's mother missed Gracie's dad.

"Yes, but—oh, I can't explain it." Tracing her daughter's outline, she ran her finger over the glass. Her ring slipped, tapped the glass.

Quite a ring the princess sported on her slim finger. Giving Jilly space and himself an outlet for the edginess building in him, Hank wandered to the door and opened it, letting it swing back again and again against the sole of his foot. "Or is it, Jilly, that you're trying to turn her into a little princess when she's nothing more than a sad little girl who's handling a difficult situation pretty well, all in all?" he said, the squeaks of the door and the slapping sound it made against his sole punctuating his comment.

"What?" Dropping her hand from the window, Jilly whipped around, facing him. Prickliness spiked from her like a baby porcupine's quills.

The door slap-slapping against his foot, he plowed on. "Well, she's a kid who likes to run. Get dirty. Yell a little. Throw a tantrum or two. Seems right normal to me. Real ordinary, in fact. Like a real kid, you know?"

"Good God. This is your analysis? I can't believe it. You think that I'm trying to turn my *child* into some plastic robot? Like one of those too-adult beauty-contest tots?" White-faced with fury, she stormed toward him. "That I'm trying to turn my daughter, my Gracie, into some *creature?* Some fairy-tale fantasy child?"

"Well, aren't you?" He let the door slam one final time. In for a penny, in for a pound, as the saying went. "Aren't you trying to cast her in your image?"

"You think I'm trying to force my child to be someone she's not?"

"Looks like that to me."

"And that I'm shutting out her grief over her father's death?" Jilly's voice trembled with outrage and distress. "You have no right to make that judgment about me."

"Think about it."

"I'm sorry. I must have missed something." Ice crackled down the line of her words. "You know about children? From vast experience, I suppose?"

"I call 'em like I see 'em."

She jabbed her index finger into his chest with each word she spoke. "That's enough. You don't have a *clue,* not a single clue, about Gracie. Or me. You sit in judgment of me and my child when you don't know a solitary thing about us. You don't know *anything!*" With one indignant thump, her finger brushed against his skin in the gap between buttonhole and button.

Hank seized her flailing hand before it poked a permanent hole in his chest. She flinched and went motionless, but her fist was a small, agitated creature in his stronger grip. "I know you smell of money, princess." Her fist still captured by his, he tapped her slim watch. "And I know that you walk like the ground's covered with a red carpet in front of you."

"How dare you?" She jerked her hand, but he held tightly to it. "How dare you make such assumptions?" Streaks of scarlet lay along her classy cheekbones, but the rest of her face was pinched white.

"And, what's more important, princess, I know that your daughter is having the time of her life grubbing in the dirt with Nicholas. Maybe she is being bossy. Maybe she's not a Victorian poster child, but she's *herself,* not some *image* of what you think a little girl should be." He let her hand drop. "That's what I know, princess, and I don't have to have a passel of kids of my own to see what's as plain as the nose on my face."

"Let me by, please." She gripped her hands in front of her and the knuckles shone blue-white. "Before I do something terrible."

"Like what, sugar? Hit me? Cry?" He hadn't meant for the subject to go so far out of control, hadn't expected his own reaction to the steady thumping of her small finger against him. But her touch had pulled the lid off his tamped-down emotions, letting loose the irritability buzzing through him. The emotions roaring forth staggered him with their intensity.

Maybe it was thinking of her husband and wanting to know more about him, maybe it was the reminder of Callie as Jilly talked about Gracie. Or maybe it was the woman herself, the way she kept spinning away from him, elusive, beguiling. Secretive.

"Hit you?" Her finger hovered above his chest.

"Go ahead. Hit away if you're angry. I can take it." He took her fist and slapped it against his chest even as she yanked her hand free. "At least it would be a real reaction, princess, not some careful gesture of social politeness that has nothing to do with what you're really thinking or feeling."

She was shaking with anger, and he wanted to grab her and pull her into his arms, wanted to lift the lid on the pressure cooker of all that anger and emotion pulsing from her and let it roll over him. Blazing with this anger that he didn't understand, he wanted all that heat turned on him.

He wanted to spear his fingers through her hair and tip her face up to his, taste her and translate that anger into a deeper, darker emotion. He wanted to show her the difference between flirting and this red darkness pounding inside him.

But he couldn't. Wouldn't.

So he stepped back.

"And if I cry?" She was tight-lipped, her fury vibrating almost visibly between them.

"Well then, I'll wipe away your tears, princess." He handed her a wadded-up bandanna from his back pocket.

She let the blue and brown square fall to the floor.

"But at least I'd know the tears were real."

"No, thank you," she said, dipping her chin to the scarf. "What you know and what you think you know are entirely different. You think you've pigeonholed me. You think you've slapped a convenient label on me. And that having done so, you *know* me. Perhaps some of what you believe is true. Sometimes I'm not sure myself anymore. But I'll tell *you* something, Hank Aaron Tyler. What you truly know about me wouldn't fill my grandmother's thimble. Now let me past." She waited for him to move back. "Please."

"Did you know that your sentences go all stiff and formal when you're feeling uncomfortable? And even in an argument, you don't forget your manners, do you, princess?" Holding the door open for her, he motioned her through.

She paused in the doorframe. "No, I don't. Manners are all that keep us going sometimes. And why is that so awful?" Her eyes were enormous and dark in her stark white face.

The emotions flooding through him made him try to spell out what he barely sensed. "Because you use those manners to cover your feelings. You hide behind them so that you don't have to deal with your real emotions. Your Gracie has a clearer idea of what she wants out of life than you do, princess."

"I can't tell you how utterly thrilled I am that you've shared that insight with me. Thank you." She brushed by him. Her elbow bumped his rib when he didn't move to give her room, and she drew her arms in close to her sides. "I'm sure you mean well."

"I meant exactly what I said about Gracie, Jilly. Think about that, too, when you get a chance." He watched her small form stalk away from him, genuine outrage in every line of her stiff spine.

And then, like a kitten played with too roughly, she whirled and sank tiny verbal claws into him. "Since you've been so generous with *your* insights, let me pass one of mine on to you. I'm not the only one who hides behind a mask."

"What do you mean?"

She grimaced, stared at the ground. "I'm sorry. I shouldn't have said anything."

Letting the door slam behind him, Hank took off after her. "What are you implying, princess?" Like a ghost, her

silvery gray shape slipped around the corner of the house
and out of sight.

"Hey, ma'am, look what me and Gracie fixed," Nicholas said.

"Mommy, where's Hank?"

"Right here, Miss Gracie."

"Oh, good." Gracie charged over to him. "Look what
me and Nickels made!"

"Nicholas and I, sweetie." Jilly's voice was soft, but
white-hot anger scorched the edges of her words.

"'kay." Gracie pulled on his hand. "C'mon, Hank. You
got to see! Mommy, show him," Gracie commanded.

Jilly was standing underneath the oak tree. A long rope
wrapped around a short board dangled from her hand. She
glanced at him hesitantly, her expression guarded, all the
wariness back in her eyes.

Hank took a steadying breath.

In her face he read as clearly as if she'd spoken out loud
her fear that their argument would spill over to her daughter. Her manners would keep her from continuing their
fight in front of the kids, but those manners were all that
kept her from turning her back on him and walking away.

He didn't want her to walk away from him.

She twisted the rope. "Gracie, leave Mr. Tyler alone,
sweetie."

In the golden October sunlight, Jilly seemed surrounded
by shadows, her narrow shoulders too slight for whatever
burdens she carried. If he could have, he would have
walked right up to her and tucked her shining brown head
against his chest, pulled her into his arms and let her rest
against him. He wished she had half the strength of her little daughter.

Standing there underneath the oak, Hank finally understood the source of his aggression. And why he kept pushing at her.

It wasn't as simple as teasing her until she came alive,
until her emotions burst through her serenity.

Yeah, he wanted to make her respond. But respond to him as a male.

Like a river channeled into a narrow gorge, a sexual craving like none he'd ever experienced was gaining increasing power over him, turning and twisting his reactions, surprising him. And underneath this frustrated hunger that he'd barely recognized was this treacherous softness, this need to protect her and give her comfort.

The twisting strands of sex and tenderness were too complicated. And he was a man who steered clear of complications.

Always. Without fail.

Talk about being hoist by his own petard, he thought. He'd tried to stir up the princess, and he'd let his own tigers loose. Well, damn it all to hell, if that didn't take the proverbial cake, chocolate or otherwise.

He'd gotten his just desserts, all right.

For both their sakes, he'd have to keep his hands off the princess.

"C'mon, Mr. Hank Tyler."

"Gracie, *please.*" Desperation shivered in the princess's tone.

"She's okay, Jilly."

"See, Mommy? Me and Hank are friends, too. He can throw the swing up." Taking his hand, Gracie hauled him forward. "Me and Nickels tried, but we couldn't make the rope go over the branch. Nickels wanted to climb up, but I said he shouldn't because it could be *very* dangerous." Looking up at the top branches, she tipped her head so far back she almost fell over. "Right?" Worry glazed her round little face. "We're not s'posed to climb that high? Right?"

"Right. You did swell, Miss Gracie." He laid his hand on top of her sun-warmed hair, its fineness so unlike the heavy silk of her mother's. "And it was probably a good idea not to climb the oak without your mom or me around. So what did y'all make?"

"A swing. I have one at home, so I knowed how to make the rope-and-board part." Nicholas took Hank's other hand. "Can you hang it from the tree? My Jake papa could. But he's not here." He skidded to a stop. "I forgot to call my mama and Jake. When are they coming to get me? Can we finish the swing and fix the horses and their feets before I go home?"

Husky and warm, Jilly's barely heard chuckle moved over his skin.

Hank glanced at her, grateful for the bridge the kids provided over the tension hissing between Jilly and him. "Well, Nicholas, we're not going to *fix* the horses, exactly. Mostly do a repair job on their—feet." Much easier to keep this unwanted craving on a tight rein when Nicholas and Gracie were around. "Hang on, Nicholas. I can hang the swing. And we don't have to hurry, because Sarah and Jake won't be here until early evening."

Silently, Jilly handed him the rope-and-board contraption.

"Thanks."

"You're welcome," she said formally and then frowned as he shot her a quick grin.

"Like I said, princess, your manners are flawless." He tapped her on the narrow bridge of her nose. "We'll talk. Later."

"Perhaps." One arm circled her waist, the other lay between her breasts with her hand resting along the curve of her neck. "But I think we've both said quite enough." The angry flush remained like red flags along her cheekbones, and her eyes were furious.

"Nope, not nearly enough. See, princess, real people argue and scrap and figure out what they think. Sort out what they want. And they even yell a little. Sometimes ... and within reason. Real people get passionate about what they're feeling, princess, and that passion shows. But when the discussing is over, they compromise. Or something. And nobody goes to war over it. Nobody gets hurt. Around our house it was called working out your differences. Getting on with the business of living."

"Scrapping and arguing. Yelling. How charming."

He grinned. She'd handed him an irresistible setup. "Can be. Depends on how they make up."

"We have nothing to settle. We had a difference of opinion. Adults do. Often. And frequently they don't know what they're talking about." Starch couldn't have made her shoulders any stiffer.

He could take a hint, especially one spelled out. "Sugar, what happened was more than a difference of opinion."

"Mr. Hank! C'mon. *Please*. Before it gets dark and Nickels goes home."

Hank glanced down at Gracie. "Hold on, honey. You and Nicholas go to the shed and find my toolbox, okay?" He pointed toward the weathered lean-to. "Nicholas knows where we keep the tools." Hank waited until they were a few feet away, and then he leaned close and lowered his voice. "Princess, maybe I spoke out of turn, and maybe I don't know beans about kids or about you and your daughter, but I'll tell you again, I meant every word I said about Gracie. You might want to chew that over in your spare moments."

"Thank you, but I doubt that I'll 'chew over' your comments." The slight tip of her head indicated that the subject was closed. Permanently, as far as she was concerned. In spite of her reluctant chuckle at Nicholas's comment, the princess was *not* amused. An ice cube would have melted next to her.

He really, really couldn't resist. And with the kids within hearing distance, a kind of safety net, he said, "As for the manner of our discussion, well, sugar—" he leaned in a little closer, invading her space good and proper "—since we keep striking sparks off each other, we're going to have to find a way of dousing the tinder, or we're going to set the forest on fire. So to speak. Think about that, too, in your spare seconds."

"Yes," she said faintly. Her hand curled into her neck. "I agree. You're right. I'll have to think about that, at least."

Seeking calm, she looked up at the cloudless blue sky where a hawk floated lazily above them, but she couldn't stop shaking inside. She wanted to take her misery, turn her back on his charming smile and run as fast and as far away from Hank Tyler as she could.

His voice deepened. "One thing more, Jilly. I want to know what you meant by your other comment, the one you tossed my way. The cutely cryptic one about masks. What did you mean, princess?"

"Nothing." She looked everywhere but at him.

"I don't believe you. You were angry. Felt pushed into a corner is what I figure, and you shoved back in your own way. And that interests me." He straightened. "And, princess, what I also reckon is that you're real skittish about letting loose your temper. You're mighty cool in general. Even when you're provoked, you shy away from confrontation. But I don't intend to let you take a pass on what you started to say."

"I'd rather drop the subject."

"I'd rather not." His drawl sounded slightly mocking to her.

"It doesn't matter. I spoke without thinking. As, possibly, you did?" She looked at him, hoping that he would agree.

He'd virtually accused her of being a failure as a mother. Yet everything she'd done as a mother had been to make sure that Gracie had as normal a childhood as possible, that she be allowed to be whoever she wanted to be. Princess, pirate or very ordinary little girl. None of that mattered as long as Gracie knew how much she was loved, loved for herself, whoever or whatever that self turned out to be.

With an eagerness that astounded her, she wanted him to laugh and deny the words piercing her heart like poisoned barbs. But he didn't. She hadn't thought he would, not really.

Her eyes smarting with anger and a deeply offended sensibility, Jilly couldn't look at him. He'd uncannily zeroed in on the deepest fears she had as a mother. How *could* he have said such things to her? To think she would want her daughter to be a little plastic doll. He couldn't possibly know how painful his accusation had been, but she was reluctant to throw his secret back in his face in retaliation.

In spite of everything that had happened, in spite of everything he'd said, she didn't want to hurt him by using his feelings about Callie Jo against him. Retaliation at that level wouldn't be fair, so, intending to end the discussion, she said, "I'm sorry that you're taking an offhand comment so seriously, but truly, it wasn't important. Let's drop it."

"I think it was. You were making a point. And we're going to come back to it. We'll talk about it. Sooner or later." His bright green gaze was too intense, disturbing her.

"Why?"

"Damned if I know, princess."

"Like an itch you have to scratch?"

"An itch?" He lifted an eyebrow. "Maybe."

"Check the medicine cabinet for calamine lotion."

"Ouch." If his grin held any humor, it was self-directed. "For some reason, I find myself interested in what you think," he said after a moment. "And in your saintly husband." He stepped to the side and his shadow fell across her. "As I said earlier at dinner, you've made me curious, princess. And that doesn't happen very often. Takes too much energy." He paused, as if surprised by his own admission. "I'm a man who likes to conserve his energy for the really important things in life."

"I'm sure you do."

"So, when I find myself in a state of...curiosity, it's well nigh impossible for me to back off, you know?"

"Do you like tearing the wings off butterflies in your free time, too? Do you need to ruin something beautiful to satisfy your curiosity?" Bitterness leaked from her voice. She didn't want him talking about Larry, not with that skeptical curl of his mouth implying... What? Something cynical and nasty.

"Why would talking about your wonderful husband ruin anything beautiful, sugar?" He didn't even move, not a muscle twitched, but suddenly he seemed to loom over her, threatening her.

She didn't want all that intensity focused on her. In the short time she'd known Hank Tyler, he'd pulled the strings of her emotions with terrifying ease, making her feel as if she were constantly on the brink of losing control.

Gripping the rectangular toolbox, Gracie and Nicholas came tearing toward them. "Hey, Mr. Hank! Look!"

As the children dropped the box on the ground and tackled Hank around the knees, he turned away from her. "Okay, cowpokes, let's see if we can tighten this rope on the board before we hang the swing."

Battered black metal box in hand, he strode back toward the tree, the kids trotting three steps to his one. "What we're going to do, see, is punch a couple of holes in this old board and put the rope through them. Be a bit sturdier that way. But you sure did a swell job tying the knots."

Jilly wanted to call after him and tell him he was wrong. They weren't striking sparks off each other. She hadn't meant anything by her careless comment. She didn't want any more encounters with him like this one they'd just had. The emotions were too strong. The mix was too rich. Destructive.

She didn't know how to cope with it. With him. The anger was too overwhelming for caution, or she'd never have said what she did. At least she'd come to her senses before she'd done permanent harm.

Somehow, Hank Tyler kept her insides churning with one unfamiliar emotion after another, turning her into a person she scarcely recognized. And, clearly, she was upsetting him.

Tomorrow she would call her lawyer and see if she could use the credit card or write checks. She was going to have to arrange a meeting with him, anyway, to find out what he had discovered. Her accounts would be freed up, and she and Gracie could leave. She wouldn't have to think about running into Hank in the hall. She wouldn't have to deal with the twinges of sympathy she felt whenever she caught glimpses of the secret he thought no one knew.

Most of all, she wouldn't have to confront the uncomfortable feelings he created in her.

She had enough to handle. She couldn't handle a green-eyed cowboy with mischief in his smile and a wounded heart.

That same green-eyed cowboy squatted on the ground with her daughter and Nicholas beside him, both imitating his movements. But the way faded white denim stretched over the long muscles of his thighs and rear end was completely adult male.

He opened his toolbox. "Y'all just didn't have the right tools to do a bang-up job on this swing." Rummaging inside, he shrugged. "Well, shoot fire, looks like I don't, either. Been so long since I've used this that I forgot what was inside. Guess we'll mosey on over to the shed again. C'mon, y'all." He stood up and lifted each child by the arm, swinging them both out in wide swoops from his body in time with their shrieks. Holding her gaze, the muscles of his arms and shoulders coiled and relaxed with each swing.

She'd never noticed a man's body the way she did Hank Tyler's. Every time he moved, his long legs strolling slow and easy, she couldn't help watching him. Her reaction was unconscious, automatic. Certainly nothing she wanted. She saw his biceps bunch up in one final outward lift of the children.

Embarrassing to be so aware of the shape of a man's muscles, the way they flexed under the bleached-out fabric of his shirt and jeans.

Disturbing to be so angry with him and yet experience this soft, melting heat in her stomach from nothing more than watching him.

Hank took the children with him to the toolshed near the corral and came back with a drill and bit. Letting each child in turn hold the drill, he showed them patiently how to bore holes in the chunky board and tie the rope in fat knots underneath.

Then, with a pocketknife, he gouged an *N* and a *G* over the hole that each had worked on. "There. For posterity." He clipped the knife shut and returned it to his pocket. "See, someday you can show your children what you made. That's important."

Tracing the letters, Gracie nodded slowly. "Me and Nickels made this. It's a forever swing, right? 'Cause trees live hundreds and hundreds of years, not like people." She bent forward over the letters. "This swing will be here forever, even if we're not?" She glanced up at the tree where a heart-enclosed *T.J. loves C.J.* showed in the bark, the wide gouges weather-darkened. "Like these 'nitials, right?"

Standing up, Hank stopped. He stooped down again, studying Gracie and giving Jilly a quick look before saying, "Yeah, sweetheart. It's a forever swing. Some things don't change. It will always be here."

Jilly's eyes stung as she watched her daughter press her finger into the channel of the *G*. "That's me. Gracie." She touched the *N*. "And Nickels." Turning her face to Hank, she dusted her hands on her bottom. "I like trees. And swings."

"Fine, Miss Gracie. I do, too. A tree is a good thing. So is a sturdy swing." He tugged Gracie's nose. "So let's make this swing operational, okay?"

Jilly wondered if he was aware of his quick glance at the initialed heart. Like dandelions, the past blew its seeds far into the present and rooted. Melancholy moved slowly through the thickness of her anger.

"We gonna need a ladder?" Nicholas handed Hank the swing seat. "I'll go get it."

"Me, too." Gracie placed a loop of rope in Hank's outstretched hand.

"Nah." He coiled the rope around his left shoulder, the board hanging under his arm as he bent his knees and leaped for the lowest branch. "I know this old oak like the back of my hand." As he hung lazily just above their heads, his shirt pulled free of his waistband, revealing a narrow strip of muscled belly. In that gap between faded shirt and worn jeans, his belly button was a narrow vertical O in smooth, brown skin.

Jilly didn't think she'd ever wanted to touch a man's skin, move her open hand across it, the way she wanted to touch that strip of sleek skin. She didn't understand the impulses building in her like a long, slow wave. She was angry with him, hurt, and still she wanted to smooth her palm across the skin showing between shirt and waistband.

Instead, she clasped her hands behind her and watched.

He shimmied up the tree, his thighs wrapping around lower branches as he stretched and pulled himself up toward the thick branch he swore was strong enough to support two swinging elephants if need be, much less two flyweight kids.

Jilly's gaze followed his path up the trunk.

And then, with an audacity that made her gasp, he swung his body out, away from the tree, building momentum for a leap from one low branch to the high one, his legs whipping him forward and across the gap. As he clung one-handed to the branch, his legs dangling high above her and the gap of skin growing increasingly wider with each second, he gave her a smart-alecky grin.

She blinked.

"Naughty, naughty, princess. If eyes could only speak—"

He knew she'd been watching him.

The devil had been engaged in a wholly different kind of teasing. With each movement of his lean body, with each reach for a branch a little out of his grasp, he'd known she was unable to look away from him.

When she didn't answer, he tossed one end of the rope over the branch with his free hand and swung closer to the dangling length of rope. Switching hands, he worked the first end into a complicated knot and then repeated the process, adjusting the knots as Gracie, hands on her hips, stood back and supervised the leveling of the seat.

"How's that, Miss Gracie?" Still dangling from the branch, he swung back and forth, his legs together, flexing at the knees for a dismount. "Like it now?"

But he was looking at Jilly.

And there was something beyond teasing in his eyes. A look that curled her insides and left her sad.

Impossible.

They both wanted something from life they were never going to find. He'd given his heart to a woman he could never have, and Jilly knew she didn't ever want to remarry.

She'd had a perfect marriage once. And it had been as perfect and rare as the fine crystal goblets she'd set on the table every night. Waiting to be filled, the glasses had shimmered under the chandelier, their cold, shining surfaces reflecting the hothouse red roses and silk draperies. All light and hard surfaces, the glasses had sparkled on the table.

Empty.

Like her.

She shivered.

The image of those sparkling glasses disturbed her profoundly.

Chapter Seven

The sun was dipping into the horizon by the time they finally went to the horse corral.

With one arm, Hank boosted Gracie onto his shoulders. "Steady, sweetheart. Easy." Gracie clasped her arms around Hank's neck in a stranglehold. "I've got you. I'm not going to drop you."

A cold lump settled in the region of Jilly's chest. She couldn't be both a mother and father, no matter how hard she tried, no matter how much she wanted to make sure that Gracie didn't sense the lack of a father.

It was more than the physical, more than energy. She had energy, for heaven's sake. She was always ready to jump rope or play volleyball—not very well, that was true—but she gave it her best effort.

What she couldn't give Gracie was the uniquely male viewpoint, the way a good man interacted with children. She couldn't give her daughter this kind of play.

But then, neither had Larry. Jilly looked down at the ground. *Neither had Larry.* She frowned.

Gracie settled securely, Hank tipped Nicholas upside down, and pedaled the boy's legs in a wheelbarrow walk until Nicholas somersaulted and lay flat out on the ground, panting.

"My turn! My turn!" Sliding off Hank's chest, Gracie collapsed in a heap at his booted feet.

"Whatever you say, Miss Gracie. Watch the sandspurs and horse-doody, though."

Nicholas chortled. "Horse-doody! My Jake papa calls it—"

"I'll just bet he does." Hank grabbed Nicholas around the middle and slung him in a fireman's carry over one shoulder. With a matter-of-fact "Oopsie-daisy," he caught Gracie's ankles and guided her in an upside-down walk on her hands across the field.

In front of Jilly, the sun turned Hank and the children into dark silhouettes as it melted into the horizon, leaving muted streaks of cloud-blurred color. The pale blue shadows and fading pink of the sky underlined her melancholy, but she didn't know why.

That was the trouble with weddings and childbirth. Postpartum was tough. She would feel better when she was back home and her affairs were settled.

She would feel much better when she didn't have to see Hank Tyler playing surrogate father to her daughter.

The thought that had struck her earlier returned as she watched Hank wheel Gracie across the pasture scrubland. Larry had never played with Gracie, never roughhoused with her, never shown her the kind of casual male affection that Hank Tyler expressed so easily. A girl needed that kind of masculine attention.

And so did a woman.

"Damn," she whispered.

For Larry, Gracie had been one more project. Gracie had learned early on to gauge her father's moods and his expectations if she wanted any of his attention, much less affection. But being Gracie, she'd found her own way of asserting her independence without withdrawing from her father.

A father was a father, after all, and Gracie had loved hers.

And, no matter what had happened, Jilly believed that Larry had loved his daughter.

Fathers and daughters. Fathers and sons. Complicated relationships that continued beyond death.

"Owie," Gracie protested. She rolled to a stop and stood up, shoving her hair back and holding up her hand to Hank.

"Aw, sweetheart, you ran over a sandspur. We'll get it out fast as a wink." Hank plunked her on the wooden fence railing. "Now hold out your palm, shut one eye at a time and count to three. Don't forget to wink each time. Got that?"

Before Gracie even began counting, Hank had flicked the spur out, his fingers flying so fast that no barbs were left, but he waited patiently as Gracie squinched first one eye, then the other and counted. "Three. Done," she said proudly, squinting one last time, thrilled with herself.

"You're tough."

"Yep." Gracie grinned up at him and patted her knee. "I have a scar from the driveway, and I *never* cried, not once."

"I would have."

Gracie looked at Hank for a long time. "I don't think so. Cowboys don't cry. It's a rule. I think."

"Yeah?" Hank lifted her off the railing. "I don't know about that, but I've cried buckets in my day."

"No!" Gracie was clearly stunned. *"Buckets?"*

"Yep." He ambled toward the gate, Nicholas walking beside Gracie this time, holding her hand and scrutinizing it for blood. "I'm the best crier in six counties. Maybe even seven."

"Was your name in the paper?"

Hank shook his head, giving an aw-shucks shrug of his shoulders and scraping the ground with the toe of his boot.

"Nope. No fame, no glory. Just a bunch of rusted old buckets, Miss Gracie. Sorry, but I'm a real disappointment, aren't I?"

Gracie reached up and patted his hand. "Yep, but it's okay. I can tell you're a real cowboy. But I would sure like to see you cry a bucket. That would be *very* interesting, Mr. Hank." Her whole body quivered with politely suppressed interest as she batted her eyelashes. "If you have time."

"We'll see." Clearly trying not to explode with laughter, Hank looked as if he'd sucked a sour lemon. "If an occasion occurs, I'll do my best."

Nicholas's expression was quizzical, but he was one hundred percent loyal. He stuck his chin out. "Jake could cry forty 'leven buckets full. If he wanted to. But he doesn't." Apparently, his Jake papa wasn't given to filling buckets with tears.

Hank nodded thoughtfully. "I'll bet he could. Easy. Heck, if he lived up here instead of down on Lake Okeechobee, I wouldn't have any chance at the record."

Jilly's melancholy deepened as she watched Hank with the two children. He enjoyed playing games with them. He delighted in their goofy points of view. He was a man who would have been a wonderful father, a man whose presence would be a gift to a child.

But unless Hank's life changed, he would never have a family of his own. He would always be on the outskirts of his brother's life, the uncle all the kids adored.

Because he would make time for them.

Because he would talk to them, tease them, treat them the same way he treated everyone. He would never make the error of talking down to them as if they were miniature aliens.

Jilly walked through the gate he opened to the horse corral and shut behind them.

He'd made a mistake about her. But he understood her daughter.

"All right, Miss Gracie, Nicholas. Sit here until I bring Baxter out. Y'all can help me, but you have to stay here until I tell you what to do. You can breathe. You can blink. Nothing else. Got that?"

Gracie nodded once, emphatically. Nicholas moved his head slowly, watching Hank stride toward a big sorrel horse near a long, open building.

Over his shoulder, Hank called back to her, "You going to be scenery, princess? Or are you coming all the way in?"

"Tell me what to do. Of course I'll help." Jilly gritted her teeth. If it weren't for Gracie, she wouldn't have stepped inside the gosh-darned fence.

He pivoted and studied her. A smile tugged one corner of his mouth. "You do scenery really well, sugar. Hop up on the fence next to my ranch hands. Or do you need some help?" he asked innocently as she scooted her behind up onto the top railing and her foot slipped.

"No. Thank you. I'm fine."

"Sure?"

She nodded decisively. "Oh, yes." She patted the railing where she perched. "Front-row seat."

Sitting on the fence was infinitely preferable to being ground-level with the four-footed creatures. She would never tell him, but it was an act of faith that she allowed her daughter and Nicholas in the corral with him. An act of faith that she trusted him with Gracie, because he had a way of being a jump ahead of the kids. He was aware of them, of what they might do.

Jilly slid her fingernail against one of the fence splinters. For a man who seemed to sail blithely along on the surface of life, Hank Tyler paid more attention to details than people realized.

If he had children, he might not know the names of their teachers, but he would know what was bothering his daughter. Or son. His child would talk to him. With words. With gestures and silences. And Hank would understand.

He would read the language of his child and know how to respond.

But he would probably never have children. The seeds of the past had sent their roots deep into him.

She blinked as light splashed onto the ground in front of them.

The white glare came from the building with its open stalls. Bridles and bits hung from nails on one wall and several worn saddles were stacked at the far end. Walking toward the sorrel horse, Hank had a plastic bowl in one hand, a metal object that reminded her of an oversize fingernail file, and a package with two containers. A halter draped over one sloping shoulder. He laid everything on the ground and motioned the children off the fence. Slipping the halter over the horse's head, he led Baxter to a fence post and looped the halter ends around the post, securing the animal's head.

Hank saw Jilly hook her feet under the second railing and lean forward. As he tied up Baxter and the kids dropped like Ping-Pong balls to the ground, her body followed them, tilting to a forty-five degree angle. Her white-knuckled hands were gripping the fence railing. Worry lines furrowed her forehead.

"You okay, Jilly?" With one hand on Baxter's satin coat, the other keeping Nicholas and Gracie clear of the horse, Hank took a step toward her.

"Wonderful. Thank you. Go right ahead." There wasn't an ounce of sincerity in her cheerful smile and quick dip of her head. "Gracie, Nicholas, listen to Mr. Tyler. Pay attention, doodlebugs."

Gracie pulled at his arm. "Mommy's afraid of horses. They're awful big. And she's worried I'll be stomped on and smashed. Or something. But she let me ride the pony at my friend Josie's birthday party. Ponies aren't big."

"I see." And he did. He'd thought Jilly didn't like the earthiness of the corral, the smells and rawness of it. He'd thought it offended her sense of delicacy. He was wrong.

The princess was in a white-faced state of terror, but she thought she was hiding it from her daughter. From him. He stooped so he was face-to-face with Gracie. "She's afraid, huh?"

"Yep, but I'm not."

He tapped Gracie's nose. "Good. Baxter wouldn't hurt a fly."

"I know." Gracie smiled sunnily at him. "He's a cow-horse."

"Sort of," Hank agreed, returning her smile. "So, you two want to see what's happened to Baxter's foot?" Toes turned in and his rear end facing the horse's rump, Hank grasped the left hind fetlock and lifted the animal's leg and hoof through his own legs, supporting it on his own bent knees. Baxter shifted, his gaskin bumping against Hank's shoulder. Hank pointed toward the sole and showed them where the hoof had splintered. "See, guys, right here along the outer wall? Baxter's hoof won't hold his shoe unless we patch up the hoof. We'll strengthen it with this dental acrylic."

"Dentist? That's for teeth, not feets." Moving closer, Nicholas touched the hard surface of the hoof.

Ten feet away, Hank saw Jilly's feet leave the railing as she slid down, staying close to the fence but moving for a clearer view. She was going to ruin those pretty gray leather shoes in the corral. Be a shame. "Watch your step, princess."

She stopped, looked down, stepped back until her back ironed the wrinkles out of the fence. "Oh."

"Horse-doody," Gracie said wisely to her mother.

"Yes, I see." Jilly's face remained sandy white, but she edged gingerly along the fence, keeping her daughter and Nicholas in view. "Go right ahead. Don't let me interrupt—"

Baxter lifted his head and looked at her. He shifted restlessly again, and Hank reached back to smooth his hand along the horse's thigh. "Easy, fella. Shh, don't get riled up. She's not going to hurt you. Besides, you're bigger. And you have four legs. She only has two. *Very* nice ones, I'll admit, but still, only two.''

Gracie giggled.

Baxter snorted.

The princess gasped, nothing more than a betraying sigh, but Hank heard it. And looked over, straight into her terrified, utterly miserable beautiful blue eyes.

She'd taken three steps forward, her hand outstretched toward Gracie to protect her from an imagined danger.

As if she weren't in a state of abject fear and standing next to horse-doody, Jilly gave him a heartbreaking smile, one filled with such do-or-die determination and unconscious courage that he wanted to pin a medal on her.

"Hey, sugar," he murmured, still standing rear-to-rear with the horse but speaking to Jilly as he clasped his hand around the horse's pastern, "Everything's fine. Baxter's just blowin' raspberries. Rude, maybe, but no big deal."

"Of course not. Good heavens, I know that," she said and the bright smile never wavered. She walked toward them, never once looking at the ground, not seeing the mud and muck that stained her shoes. "I thought I might give you all a hand, that's all."

He knew in that moment exactly where Gracie's stubborn independence came from. Jilly and her daughter were two peas in a pod.

Damned if the princess wasn't a warrior woman in disguise. He wondered if she realized how brave she was.

"Here, sugar, you hold the bowl." With a free hand, he snagged the plastic margarine bowl and handed it to her, keeping her well out of Baxter's curious head turns. "Gracie, you and Nicholas are going to mix up this acrylic that we're going to use to fill in ol' Baxter's hoof." He gave the pink powder to Gracie and handed Nicholas the clear liquid.

Gazing at the fluffy pink powder, Gracie held the four-ounce jar with both hands. "Baxter's a boy."

"More or less."

Hoping to make Jilly give him a real smile, one that would show she was finally relaxing, he murmured, "You can explain *this* part, sugar, because what Baxter is, is a gelding."

"Fine. No problem. Whatever you say." Hank decided Jilly hadn't registered anything he'd said yet.

Gracie tipped the bottle back and forth. "Daddy always said pink was for girls. Pink will look funny on Baxter."

"My buddy, Dr. Pokorny, didn't have any clear or blue acrylic on hand, so Baxter's going to be handsome in pink. He'll never know, sweetheart." In a low voice meant only for Jilly's ears, Hank added, thinking it might get a rise out of her, "And no, sugar, I wasn't making some male chauvinist statement when I gave Gracie the jar of pink stuff. I picked up the acrylic first, that's all."

"Very nice. Good idea." No longer rosy red, her mouth was pale, her eyes glazed as she concentrated on Gracie and Nicholas. Her gaze kept slipping toward Baxter.

"Glad you approve." Hank didn't know whether to laugh or swear. Jilly hadn't heard a word he said. He doubted that she even knew what a gelding was, or that he was trying to make a joke about the pink acrylic. Her every sense was on the alert. And, in spite of her fear, she was ready to snatch either child out of harm's way.

"Are we going to pack the material into the hoof? That should be interesting." Jilly's phrase echoed her daughter's refrain.

Hank decided that in Jilly's case, *interesting* served as a verbal space holder, but when Gracie used it, *interesting* accurately reflected the small dynamo's thoughts.

"Yep." He made his voice as soothing for Jilly as he would have for one of the mares about to foal. "We're going to smooth it right in here, between the outer well and the white line so that it will give us something to nail the shoe into."

"Nails. Great." Her face went a pale green, but her voice was rock-steady as she leaned down to Gracie. "When we go home, you'll have a lot to talk about, won't you, doodlebug?"

"Yes. And I'll make the whole class be quiet and listen. They'll want to know about Baxter's shoes." Gracie stuck one chubby hand into her mother's.

"Perhaps Hank will give you a horseshoe? You could take it to school." Soft and controlled, brave, Jilly's voice spiraled inside him, touching him in a long-forgotten place as she looked down at her daughter.

"Sure thing, Miss Gracie," he said. "Nicholas, too." As Hank stood up, a line from an old high school play slipped into his thoughts, something about the valiant only tasting of death once but cowards dying many times before their deaths.

Maybe he had the idea backward, but it seemed to him that it was the other way around. Sure, there was damned-fool ignorant courage. The kind of courage that propelled you into danger when you didn't know the consequences. But it seemed to him that it took more backbone to know what you were facing and not look away from what you needed to do.

That was *courage.*

Valiant. It was a good word for the woman who, white-faced and smiling, faced him with her child's hand in hers.

Watching them, he was struck by the picture they made. Hand in hand, the girl-child who faced the world fearlessly, and the woman who, knowing what the worst could be, made herself walk right through her fears for love of her child.

He was oddly moved that Jilly had trusted the children in the corral with him at all. He'd accused her of trying to stifle Gracie's exuberance. He owed the princess an apology.

She had a quiet, inner strength he hadn't recognized. He'd underestimated her.

"What do we do now?" Taking a determined step forward, Jilly thrust the margarine container toward him. Without her high heels on, she barely came to the top of his chest. The off-center part in her shiny dark hair gleamed whitely in the light from the stalls, stirring him with its vulnerability.

"Well, sugar, Miss Gracie's going to dump her powder into that bowl you're holding—yep, go ahead, Gracie—" Keeping Baxter's leg on his own, Hank braced the jar against his chest and unscrewed the lid with one hand. "Then Nicholas is going to put the monomer in." He showed Nicholas how to pour about a third of the clear liquid into the bowl. "Stir it up three times, Nicholas, and then let Gracie mix it."

"It's hot!" Wide-eyed, Nicholas hunched his shoulders. His mouth was stretched in an upside-down grimace of dismay. "It's going to burn us up!"

"Nah." Hank stuck his finger into the mixture as Nicholas handed over the metal kitchen knife to Gracie. "Feel." He let Nicholas poke the pink claylike lump. "Chemistry. You mix two unlikely substances together and sometimes you get heat. A chemical reaction." From under the lock of hair falling in his eyes, he shot a look at Jilly. That was what was happening with him and the princess. Two unlikely people producing heat. Chemistry of an altogether different kind. A heat he wasn't prepared for. Hank cleared his throat. "Okay, Miss Gracie. Stir it a couple of times."

She tentatively stirred the knife before giving him a questioning glance as one short finger hovered over the acrylic-caked container.

"Yeah, go ahead. You can touch it. It's not going to burn you. If there's any acrylic left that hasn't set up, I'll give it to you and Nicholas. You can shape it into something."

"Really?" Gracie's eyes were enormous. "Oh, *thank* you, Mr. Hank." She slap-slapped the knife vigorously against the side of the plastic bowl and gave it back to him.

Steadying Baxter's leg again, Hank lifted the metal rasp and swept it against the hoof, filing away the ragged pieces. "See, here's a place where the hoof has broken away. The acrylic will be like a patch, rebuilding it."

Gracie and Nicholas leaned over his shoulder. In his peripheral view, Jilly's right foot inched forward, then her left. *One more, princess.* He wanted her to be part of what they were doing, and he felt a sense of pride as step by step, she approached them. *Good girl.*

He gave a final rasping stroke against the hoof, tested the acrylic and showed Nicholas and Gracie how to push it into the space, building up the hoof. "Want to try, sugar?" He held the acrylic-laden knife out to Jilly.

"No, thank you." Her hands were behind her back, her face bleached out by the harsh light, but she wasn't retreating. She was there. With them. "You have two helpers already. Another time, perhaps."

Gracie looked at him and rolled her eyes.

He choked back a laugh. The kid was way too precocious. Jilly had her work cut out for her, that was for sure. And the princess was absolutely clueless that her daughter had her pegged to an inch. Gracie knew exactly how hard her mother was working to keep up a brave front.

He hoped that in years to come, Gracie would appreciate her mother. And, even though his instincts told him otherwise, he hoped that Larry Elliott had known what kind of woman he'd married. No matter what else her husband had been, he'd also been one lucky son-of-a-gun. Luckier than he deserved, probably. A primitive instinct hinted that no matter how much Jilly painted him in saintly colors, Larry Elliott hadn't been quite the picture of perfection.

Hank was stunned by how much he wanted to believe Saint Larry had real big feet of clay.

Anyone Jilly loved would never be alone. In her quiet way, she would be there at that person's side, no matter what it cost her personally. With a certainty beyond proof, he knew that about her.

Now, standing behind him, her presence only a pencil-thin shadow on the ground, a drift of fragrance over the night air, she brushed her hand across Gracie's shoulder.

That tiny, revealing movement pierced him to the heart. Made him realize how empty his life was. He had no one to come home to at night, no one to carve initials in swings for.

"Okay, folks—" he touched the patch job "—the acrylic has hardened, so let's shoe Baxter." He gestured to the metal horseshoe and box of shoe nails. "I'll do the first one, but y'all will have a turn."

"Won't the horse kick?" Jilly's whisper was so quiet he almost missed it.

"He's secured. I'll have the kids on this side, away from his free leg. I won't let anything happen to them, Jilly." He reached out his finger and touched the curve of her chin, let his finger stay a heartbeat too long before he grasped Baxter's foot again with both hands. "I promise."

"I know you know what you're doing, but thank you." The relief in her voice went beyond politeness and changed the phrase into something personal.

Equally grave, Hank nodded. "You're welcome, Gillian Elliott."

He angled the first nail in, let the kids try their hand until, one by one, the nails secured Baxter's shoe and Hank released the horse's leg, giving it one final pat. Reaching deep into his pocket, he pulled out three sugar cubes and let Nicholas and Gracie give Baxter his treat.

Before untying the halter, he motioned them out of the way. Never taking her eyes off the horse, Jilly had both children close to her and was backing toward the fence.

"Anybody want to check out Baxter's new shoe?"

"Me!"

"Me, too!" Gracie pulled Jilly's arm forward, but Jilly didn't lose her grip on the child.

Casually, Hank turned the horse to face them. "Good boy," he said, patting Baxter's muzzle. "He's about as temperamental as a potato. Not a very exciting ride," he added for Jilly's benefit.

"I'm so sorry to hear that." A trace of humor dusted her face with color. "What a shame. I'm not sure we'll get over the disappointment. Personally, I was looking forward to a fast gallop around the corral. Or even outside. In the wide-open spaces." Indicating the scrubland beyond the fence, she made a circling motion with her hand firmly gripping Gracie's.

"I know, I know, Baxter and I have let you down, but what can a poor cowboy do? You know the cowboy's code won't allow him to put anything above his horse, and old Bax has been around a long time. We've grown attached to him, even if he isn't built for speed. So we make do." Hank patted Jilly on the shoulder in much the same casual way he'd given Baxter his atta-boy. "Pick a number, sugar, between one and ten. Winner goes for a ride first."

Nicholas picked five, Gracie nine and Jilly said the number was three, so Nicholas went first. Plopping him on the horse in front of him, Hank gave him a big squeeze and wrapped an arm securely around his waist.

Nicholas wiggled around to stare at him. "No saddle?"

"Nope."

"Good."

"All right, squirt, let's ride the high country."

"Yep, ride 'em," Nicholas agreed, slapping his leg. "Go, Baxter, go!" Nicholas thumped his heels against the horse's shoulders.

"See you later, ladies." Nudging Baxter forward, Hank made an imaginary tip of his hat to Jilly and Gracie. "I've missed you, monkey. You having fun with Gracie?"

The boy nodded and bounced once. "Lots. It's the greatest. I like Gracie. She likes to do things. And I like the ranch." Then he leaned back against Hank's chest. "But I miss my mommy and Jake. And they miss me, too. They need me.''

"I'll bet they do."

"Yep." There was utter confidence in his short nod. "Lots. 'Cause I am their boy."

"If I had a boy like you, squirt, I'd miss him, too." Hank was crazy about the kid, had been since the first time he'd seen him. He was such a big-eyed, solemn tadpole, and he'd been through too much.

Four years ago, the whole family had been devastated with grief when Sarah was informed by the State Department that Nicholas had been killed with his father in a Mideast bombing. Now they all tried extra hard to make up for the years that they'd never have.

Nicholas drummed his heels energetically. "Faster!"

"Okay. If you're sure."

Nicholas's head bobbed up and down like one of the dashboard dogs' heads. "Go like the wind."

"Hang on. We're shifting into overdrive if Bax can stand the pace." Hank kneed the horse into a smooth gallop, guiding him with legs and knees around and around the corral.

Jilly and Gracie were perched on the fence watching them, and when he decided Nicholas's turn was up, he rode over beside them. Jilly blanched as they approached, but she didn't move as Hank lifted Nicholas off the horse and onto the fence railing.

Scooping Gracie up quickly, Hank guided Baxter away from the fence and back around the corral.

Gracie's smile was ecstatic as he set her down in front of him, her short legs sticking straight out to the sides. "I love Baxter," she crooned, leaning forward and flattening herself against the horse's neck. Her tiny butt was a denimed bump on the red of the horse's coat. "He's the sweetest old thing." She patted the horse gently. "And he likes me, too."

"Oh?" Hank was intrigued. "How can you tell?" Maybe it was a female-intuition thing, one of those things his mama always referred to that he and Buck and T.J. had never figured out.

Sitting up straight, Gracie twisted toward him and frowned. "Mr. Hank, you're teasing me. Like you tease my mommy, aren't you?"

Hank grinned. "Not quite, Miss Gracie."

"Well, I can tell Baxter likes me because he has *very* expressive eyes. They're the window to his soul. And Baxter has a *beeyootiful* soul," she chanted. "Beeyootiful, beeyootiful Baxter horse." She leaned forward again and rubbed her cheek against the animal's neck. "I'm going to be a cowboy, Mr. Hank. When I am much bigger. 'Cause then I will buy Baxter and he will be my cowhorse, and we will live together on a ranch somewhere and wear cowboy boots." She lifted one sneaker-clad foot. "Boots are better for ranches, you know."

"I've heard that. We'll see if we can scare up a pair of Gracie-size boots for you to wear while you're here."

"Really? Truly?" She looked as though he'd given her Barbie, the dream house and Ken all at once. "Real cowboy boots? For me?"

"Sure." Hank click-clicked his tongue and guided the horse into a gallop along the back side of the corral. As the horse rounded the circle, Hank looked over his shoulder and saw Jilly's expression.

Even though her arm was around Nicholas, she looked left out, somehow forlorn as she sat there in her shimmery gray slacks and shirt. Hooked around the bottom railing, her leather-clad feet anchored her to the fence, but she leaned forward, toward them, longing visible in every curve of her body, in every dreamy flicker of her misty eyes.

Hank twitched the halter ends against Baxter's neck. Jilly's spirit said go, but her fear chained her to the fence, kept her on the other side of an experience some hidden part of her soul craved. He understood that kind of longing. It was what had led him to flying airplanes through rainstorms, hailstorms and around tornadoes. He could see the yearning in the gentle downward curve of her lips, in the way they parted wistfully at Gracie's whoop of joy.

And all that yearning spoke to him, touched him. He wanted to see her face burning with wonder, not pinched with fear.

Horses scared the princess senseless, but she wanted to be part of the party, too. Well, damn him for a fool, but if the princess wouldn't come to the party, he'd bring the party to her.

Slowing Baxter to a sedate walk, he returned Gracie to her mother. "Your turn, princess," he said, leaning forward over the horse's shoulder.

"No, thank you. I'm not—not very athletic. I would fall off." Her words sputtered forth. "I've never been good at sports."

"Baxter isn't a sport. He's a horse. Old. Placid. Mild-mannered. A gentleman of a horse, princess."

"Oh, no, I couldn't. Really, I can't. Horses—"

"Baxter's very sweet, Mommy. Me and you could ride sometime. P'rhaps." There was an adult sadness in Gracie's voice. She didn't expect anything of the sort to happen.

But Jilly studied her daughter's face, Hank's, and then reached out her hand and quickly tapped Baxter's nose, saying, "Nice horse." She yanked her hand back as he whuffed.

Hank steadied the horse as he considered her. The princess was caught between can't and wish-I-could. He reckoned he would give her a nudge in the direction he sensed she really wanted to go. "Double-dog-dare you, sugar."

"What?" She drew back as Baxter sidled closer.

Hank leaned over until his face was inches from hers. Lifting an eyebrow, he said, "Nobody can refuse a double-dog-dare, princess. It's the rule. Remember? Or didn't you ever play by schoolyard rules? Did you cheat, maybe?"

Her eyes glinted. "I remember. I never cheat."

"Well, shucks, you're not a scaredy-cat, are you?" He rested his flattened palm along Baxter's side. "I mean, a *scaredy-cat?* That's awful, princess. How're you going to hold your head up if that news gets out?"

"Pride, Hank Aaron Tyler. Pride. It can make you do anything you have to."

As the shadow passed over her face, he damned himself for being a forgetful fool. Jake had hinted that maybe there was something not quite right about Saint Larry's accidental death. Something not quite right about Saint Larry himself.

Maybe Jake was right.

Chapter Eight

Hank decided that sometimes a guy just had to thrash on through the brambles, willy-nilly. And while he wasn't inclined to exert that kind of energy as a rule, something about the princess kept him from smiling regretfully and walking away from her. Damned if he could remember the last time he'd put this much energy into anything except flying. Or sleeping.

He sighed. Hell's bells, he didn't give this much emotional energy to his occasional romantic episodes. Shoot, he couldn't back off now, not after a double-dog-dare. He let Baxter sidle an inch or two closer to the railing.

"So live a little dangerously, princess. Besides, you don't strike me as a wuss. Your knight-at-arms awaits." He crooked his arm toward her in a fake chivalric pose as he leaned right over her and whispered, "And there is that matter of the double-dog-dare."

She bit her lip. "I can't, I can't," she finally whispered. "You don't understand—"

The white line around her mouth spoke of a fear beyond reticence, beyond adolescent awkwardness. It was a fear he didn't have the heart to continue fighting. "Jilly, it's all right. You don't have to. I was only—hell. The three of us were having a good time. You weren't. I wanted to include you." He shrugged and straightened, intending to take Baxter back to the stall and settle him down for the night. "That's all."

Fear and true grit and that steely core he'd seen once or twice already battled to a standstill in her face. Grit and steel won. "I'll do it."

"Yay, Mommy!" Gracie clapped her hands.

"Right. Hop on, sugar." Hell, he wasn't going to give her time to think. He took both of Jilly's cold hands in his and swung her up and sideways in front of him, steadying her with an arm around her narrow waist as she worked her leg over and faced front. She was shaking and he could hear her teeth chattering. Damn his impulses. He should have kept his mouth shut. That blasted streak of bravery had surfaced and maybe he'd let the princess jump in over her head. "You okay?"

"Yes, thank you." Her teeth clicked shut. She turned her head to Nicholas and Gracie who were clapping and cheering. "This is great!" Her lips stuck to her teeth, and she was rigidly upright, her rounded bottom plunked firmly against the vee of his jeans, right up against the seams. Right against the zipper.

He figured she was concentrating too damned hard on being brave to notice. But he did. Oh, he noticed, all right. And felt like the jerk of all times under the circumstances for liking the way her rear end settled snugly against him.

Urging Baxter into a trot, Hank tried to think of anything and everything except the way Jilly's bottom bounced, jounced and smacked against the horse. Against him.

He told himself that if she'd leaned into the horse's rhythm, moved with the horse, with *him*, it would have been easier to ignore the shape of her jolting against him. He tried to ease back, to give her space, to give himself breathing room, but she bumped once, hard, as Baxter broke stride and Jilly's sweet little rump slapped right back in place.

Every tense line of her shouted to him that she was trying damned hard not to let fear send her into a screaming, whimpering fit. But like her tuneless, endearing singing, she didn't have a clue.

He knew she was afraid, and he didn't want her to think he was criticizing, but he knew he had to do something. It didn't seem right somehow to be breaking into a sweat every time her spine slipped against his chest or her rear end bumped hard against his jeans. Seemed a bit like taking advantage of her, but he was damned if he could figure out what to do that wouldn't embarrass her or hurt her feelings.

And he wasn't altogether sure he was quite noble enough to head Baxter back to the stall. Not . . . just . . . yet.

Bump and bumpbump.

"Uh, Jilly, sugar," he muttered, calling on every last remnant of nobility residing in his body, "reckon you can think of riding as being kind of like dancing?"

"What?" She was breathless. She didn't move, didn't turn to look at him. Her posture remained board-stiff, every muscle tensed and shaking.

"Move with the rhythm? Feel?" He placed one of her hands on Baxter's shoulder. "See? Move with him. Like dancing," he encouraged as her rump shifted against him. "You can dance, can't you, princess?"

Impossible, but her spine grew even straighter. "Yes, I can dance. And I can move with this damn horse's rhythm." Spoken through clenched teeth, her words came softly back to him with the whip of her hair against his mouth, the satin smoothness clinging to his evening beard.

"Good," he grunted and brushed away the slippery strands.

She made an effort, but the more she tried, the worse it got. For him. For her.

And for poor old Baxter who wasn't used to the kind of off-rhythm, bouncing rider Jilly was. Once Baxter whinnied in a kind of reproachful horse complaint, and Jilly's shoulders bowed and her legs went stiff, her knees poking into Baxter, and then Hank could see her forcibly make herself go into her version of relaxed.

She might walk on money, she might never have worked a day in her life, but somewhere, somehow, the princess had developed courage, that was for sure.

He admired her courage. And he liked too damn much the feel of her against him.

Hank wished he'd listened to good sense, wished she were someone else, anyone else at that moment as her fanny snuggled into the spread of his legs and her breast brushed against his arm. If she were anyone else, there would be an easy, pleasant solution to the sting of need pulsing through him.

And if she were Callie Jo—

Well, she wasn't.

"Here, princess." Hank wrapped the halter around her hand with his. "We're going to speed up." Maybe a faster pace would distract her, give him other things to think about.

Jilly's back stiffened.

"Only a little. Try to relax into the flow of Baxter's movements. Keep one hand on the halter with mine, the other on Bax's shoulder. Don't think about anything except how his muscles feel under your hand, how the wind feels against your face. See how nice the old fella moves?" Gripping with his knees and legs, he signaled Baxter into a canter, then a gallop.

"Oh. Goodness," she said, and her hand tightened against his, her fingers clinging.

They circled twice, smoothly, the wind a damp caress on their skin, the scents of horse and night mingling in a rich perfume that spoke to him of the past, of times that never were, never could be again.

He'd missed the ranch, missed his home.

"See what a goer Bax is? See how he moves, like oil across water?" A tang of orange blossoms drifted to him, blended with the forest-flower fragrance of the princess as he used his knees to press hers against the horse, to give her a feeling of what Baxter could do. Jilly's long thighs matched his, gray fabric glimmering against the worn denim over his thighs.

And suddenly, the princess had it.

Her body moved with Baxter's, with his, in a smooth, powerful rhythm that sent the blood pounding through his veins and made him reckless, made him surrender to the cool sweetness of the moment, of the night. Her hair tangled again in his beard-rough skin, tickling his nose, teasing his mouth, and this time he let it stay. Her narrow shoulders relaxed, her spine curved against him and he heard her gasp as Baxter straightened out on the curve and soared over the gate.

They raced around the stall and back over the gate and headed to the darkness gathering in the corner of the corral, Baxter a warm, powerful engine under them, speeding them through the cool, damp October night. Under his palm, her ribs moved with her breathing, and he was joined with her in that rhythm of horse and breath and night.

With each drumming stroke of Baxter's hooves against the earth, Hank's heart thundered and his arms tightened around Jilly, a woman who tempted him to forget the shadow in his heart.

But under the recklessness, under the loneliness, there was always the knowledge that he had to live with himself, had to face himself in the mirror.

He knew what the reality of his life was, what it would be.

When he slowed the horse to a walk in the gloom at the edge of the stalls, Jilly leaned back against him and sighed.

"I didn't think I could do it." She was silent for a long moment as Baxter plodded back to Nicholas and Gracie whose chatter carried lightly to them on the rising night wind. "But I did. And I enjoyed it more than anything I can remember in a long, long time." She sighed again.

Before they turned the corner and came into view of the kids, she turned carefully to him, lifted her right arm and curled it around his neck. Rising slightly so that her face, pale and soft-eyed, came up out of the darkness toward him, she whispered, "Thank you. You don't know what this meant to me." And then, like a breeze ruffling the surface of the gulf, she kissed him, a soft press of her lips against his.

Hank knew she meant it to be a social kiss aimed for his cheek, a Hollywood kind of social face-pressing, but Baxter danced sideways, and Hank glanced down. Jilly's mouth met his, tender, warm, feminine in its curves and smoothness.

He should have left it at that, but he couldn't. There wasn't that much nobility left in him. Beguiled by the touch of her, intrigued by her, he slanted his mouth across hers, taking what she offered so sweetly. She sighed once more, tipped her head, and Hank gathered the ends of the halter in one hand and cupped the back of her head with the other. His fingers slipped through the satiny stuff of her hair as they curled around the lovely shape of her head.

Lost in the taste and texture of her mouth opening under his, he was dimly aware of the sound of Gracie and Nicholas, dimly aware of distant car lights heading up the approach to the house.

He was nineteen again, home, and his body alive as it had never been before or since. The long, lonely years were gone. Or maybe they'd never existed. Maybe nothing had ever been except this moment. But the emptiness inside him melted, vanished. Wonder filled him as her fingers stroked the side of his neck. "Oh, sweetheart," he whispered back, the silence a blanket of intimacy. "Come here." He gath-

LINDSAY LONGFORD   141

ered her closer, tight against his chest, breathing in the sweetness of her skin, her hair, *her.*

For a second, in that instant as he deepened the kiss and the world shrank to the woman in his arms, he forgot everything, knew only that he was *home,* that the long years of self-exile were over.

He groaned as he pulled her closer, needing *something* in that moment, seeking something that he couldn't even put a name to.

But a car honked, Nicholas shrieked, "Mommy, Jake!" and the world rushed in again and Hank found himself looking down into dazed, dusky blue eyes and wondered for a bitter moment if he'd been kissing Jilly or Callie.

Appalled with himself, he jerked away, the ends of the halter slipped through his fingers and Baxter galumphed for the fence. He shook his head over and over again, and then, once, touched his fingers to Jilly's lips in regret, in apology.

Her hand no longer wrapped in the halter under Hank's, she faced front, head down, and gripped Baxter's mane.

On the other side of the fence, Nicholas and Gracie were scrambling down, Nicholas racing toward his parents and Gracie trotting along behind him.

Jilly was rigid in front of Hank, her shoulders hunched as if he'd hit her.

He wanted to say something, but there was nothing to say. It had been more than a kiss, more than an invitation to that pleasurable dance of male and female. Confusion muddied his thinking. He didn't know what had happened. All he knew was something had changed, shifted, in that long moment when he'd held Jilly close to him, her heart beating fast against the runaway beat of his.

"Hey there, Hank! Did my tiger give you any grief?" Sarah had Nicholas wrapped in her arms.

"How you doing, sport? Missed you." Jake was plastered around both Sarah and Nicholas, his saturnine face lit with a rare smile. "Have fun?"

They were a threesome. A family. Created by fate, fortune and passion, they had come together, forged bonds that would endure through the years.

"Hey, Jake, Sarah," he said, waving a hand. "Nicholas was fine. A big help, in fact. Be with you in a minute." The longer he looked at the three Donnellys, the more his throat closed in on him. Not even realizing it, they formed a closed circle of love, of family.

Of everything he'd sacrificed.

He lifted Jilly off the horse and onto the fence. He didn't know what she would say. What she would do. He expected anger. Embarrassment. That she'd be offended. Haughty.

He didn't expect the wistful smile as she raised her small hand and laid it against his cheek, the warm touch a caress and an unwanted comfort. He didn't expect the soft pity that deepened and darkened her eyes.

He turned Baxter away and headed through the darkness to the bright glare of the stall.

He'd never kissed Callie. Never touched her. Yet, there had been that sense of familiarity, of *homecoming,* when he'd kissed Jilly and forgotten everything in those moments of wild impulse.

Stopping, he glanced over his shoulder toward Jilly.

As she climbed down the other side of the fence and walked toward the Donnellys and Gracie, he didn't expect and didn't understand the desolation grinding inside him like broken glass.

He was in the darkness. Alone.

Well, he'd made his choices. He'd done what he had to. He knew that. He'd always known that fact, even at nineteen. And for the first time since he'd said his lying, cheerful farewell to the ranch and his family, he wanted what he'd given up.

Wanted *something.*

* * *

The taillights of the car winked down the road, vanished, and Jilly drew a deep breath. Her mouth burned with the lingering touch of Hank's kiss, and her whole body vibrated with the rush of blood, of *life*, through her veins.

The wind had picked up, bringing with it the smell of ozone and the taste of rain.

Hank had come back to say goodbye to the Donnellys, but he'd been unusually quiet, remote. It was as though the Donnellys had taken something with them when they left. Nicholas's thin face pressed against the rear window of the black pickup was a ghostly shape in the darkness, and Gracie took five running steps toward him before coming to a drooping halt, her face forlorn.

"I miss Nickels already, and he isn't even gone," she wailed as Jilly picked her up.

"I know, snickerdoodle. I know." Tucking Gracie's tear-stained face into her shoulder, Jilly carried her back to the ranch house. "You'll feel better tomorrow. I promise."

"But Nickels won't be here." Gracie hiccuped once and then was silent as Jilly carried her through the yard and toward the house.

Shining warmly through the cool night, the yellow lights welcomed them out of the darkness. Stepping onto the porch and walking through the shabby living room with its faded slipcovers and muted colors, Jilly felt like an imposter. It was a house where the very boards seemed to breathe with a life of their own, a life where love had been given, returned—*shared*—and traditions had been handed down over generations. It was more than a building.

It was a home.

And, for the thousands and thousands of dollars spent on it, her Naples house had never been that. Never been a home.

She'd never realized it until now.

She would sell the thing once her lawyer had straightened out whatever was going on with her funds.

But no matter what else happened in the coming days, she'd learned something about her life, herself, tonight. She'd been asleep all those years of her marriage and never known that, either. A perfect house. A perfect marriage.

But all surface perfection with no substance. That was why she'd been so disturbed by the image of the crystal glasses. Strange, she thought as she helped Gracie brush her teeth, how a woman could buy into an illusion, spend her energies polishing it and never know the shining reflection was false.

A mirage. She'd seen what she wanted to see. What she needed to see.

Would she ever have realized what a pale imitation of life her marriage had been?

Had there been nothing there on her part except her guilt? Guilt that Larry had worked so hard to create a wonderful life for them, giving up so much for her, and yet she hadn't been able to give him what he deserved?

Was that what had kept their marriage going? *Guilt?*

There was a question she suspected would keep her awake.

As she tucked Gracie into bed, she saw Hank's shadow pass in the hall, and continue toward his room.

They weren't going to talk about what had happened. She knew that.

She knew, too, why he triggered her anger, her emotions. He made her *feel,* feel alive, feel electrified with emotions and yearnings.

And, in an odd way, she was grateful to him. He'd shown her the possibilities in front of her. When she'd been lost and not even known it, he'd taken her to a place where dreams were possible, where they might become real. No, they couldn't talk about what had happened. But she would remember. And make her life different from now on.

"Good night, Gracie," she whispered, brushing her daughter's forehead with a kiss. "I love you, sweetie, more than anything in the whole wide world."

"Love you, too, Mommy," Gracie murmured sleepily and turned over, her doll clutched in one grubby fist.

Showered, barefoot and in clean, wrinkled jeans, Hank was in the dimly lit hallway, leaning against the wall when she shut Gracie's door. Wet and swept back off his forehead, his hair was dark brown, making him look older and harsher.

"Nice," he said, glancing toward the closed door, his expression as blank as the door in front of them. His shoulders cast a wide vee of shadow against the wall. "Mother and child."

Jilly shrugged.

"You love her more than anything in the world, huh?"

"Of course." She didn't know how to answer him, how to explain the irrevocability of her love for her child. That love had astonished her with its intensity and fierceness. She didn't understand it herself. How could she explain it to him? It was simply a given in her life. The alpha and omega of her being. "I would do anything for her. Why?"

"Just curious, princess, that's all."

He reminded her of a cat playing with a mouse. "Good night, Hank." She turned to go to the bedroom she was using.

Not touching her, he stopped her with a question. "Why were you so surprised that you were able to ride Baxter? I've been thinking about that. You were terrified, weren't you?"

"Yes." She clasped her hands in front of her. "I'm not anymore. Again, thank you."

Closing his wide hand around her arm, he turned her to face him. "Why were you so frightened? I watched you, you know. You wanted to ride. You wanted to protect Gracie and Nicholas, and you were about the color of a bleached-out lime."

"Oh, thank you so much for the lovely picture." She looked down at the feet-polished old boards of the hall floor. "I'll be sure to record it in my memory book."

"It's true." He shifted, coming to her side. Their shadows formed a sideways T along the wall. His voice was gentle. "Why, princess? Tell me."

"All right." She glanced down at his brown fingers against her shirtsleeve. Their warmth and strength penetrated the thin fabric. Strong, powerful hands. Hands that had protected her child. Hands that had held hers and shown her that she could find her own strength, her own pleasure. "Horses."

"Yes," he said encouragingly. "Four-footed critters."

She struggled to find the easiest way to tell him so that his curiosity satisfied, he would let her pass. "I lived with an older cousin from the time I was seven."

"Why?" His free hand lifted the hair caught in the collar of her blouse. He left his hand there, at the back of her neck where her nerve endings tingled.

Outside, the rain came in with a rush, pounding on the roof, slashing against the windows.

She lifted her head. "My father was a horse trainer in Kentucky. My mother was riding one of the two-year-olds he was training. I was watching her ride one day."

His hand tightened around the nape of her neck. "And?"

"She was pregnant. She fell. Possibly she was feeling light-headed, dizzy. I never knew. No one ever told me. Her foot tangled in the stirrups."

His fingers stirred against her neck.

A gust of wind slammed a door shut. She jumped.

Hank's fingers stroked her neck, soothing her. "Go on."

"It's a short story. Not much to tell. My father tried to free her. He couldn't. The horse was confused, frantic. It rammed him against a stone wall. I saw his head hit the wall, saw my mother roll under the hooves."

"Aw, Jilly." He drew her head to his chest.

Steadying herself, she inhaled. He smelled of soap and shampoo and fabric softener.

"What else?" His palm slid once down her spine, slow and sweet, and then up again.

"That's it." She exhaled. "And I went to live with my very, very wealthy cousin who had more money than she knew what to do with and no interest in a silly seven-year-old." Jilly swallowed past the lump in her throat. She was so tired. If she could, she'd sleep for a week.

"And yet you let Gracie ride with me? After all that?"

"I have to." In spite of the wave of tiredness swamping her, Jilly tried to inject the certainty she felt into her voice. "I don't want her burdened with my fears. And I take pride in the fact that she's not."

"No. She's utterly fearless."

"Good." Jilly hadn't told anyone the story in so long that she'd forgotten its power to hurt. Her eyes burned.

"And that's why you were ticked off with me when I said you were trying to turn her into your own image?" His face was grim.

"I suppose." Exhaustion suddenly drained her.

"I'm sorry, princess."

"For what?" Wearily she lifted her head to look into his somber eyes.

"For everything. For your lost childhood. For being an idiot and thinking I understood what was going on between you and your daughter. For being so pompous as to give advice where none was wanted. Or needed. You've done a good job with Gracie, Jilly. She's a swell kid." He placed a finger under her chin, tipped it up, made her look him in the face. His smile was as warm as sunshine on an April morning. "A swell kid, even if she is a shade bossy."

Jilly dipped her head, tears burning her eyes.

"But I was right about one thing. One thing I won't recant."

"What's that?" Even to her own ears, her voice sounded rusty.

"You *were* trying to make her in your own image—the image of a courageous woman. And someday, if she's lucky, she'll have a tenth of your courage and strength. Good night, Gillian.''

He dropped his hand and walked away from her, down the long hall to his room. He shut his door quietly behind him.

In the silence and shadows of the hallway, Jilly missed his touch, missed its silent message of understanding.

She went to her bedroom, shutting the door as silently behind her as he had. And all night long, she thought about unanswerable questions, about her future.

In the morning, Hank handed her a green pinecone about two inches long. A pair of miniature cowboy boots dangled from one hand. "You didn't have to make up my bed, Jilly. I told you I'd take care of whatever I needed.''

"Making a bed doesn't take long. It was no trouble.'' Baffled, she took the scratchy cone. "Thanks.'' She laid it on the kitchen table.

"I thought you left it in my bed for me.'' He picked up the pinecone and tossed it in the air, catching it and tossing it over and over as he stared at her. "I thought you were leaving me some kind of message.''

"A pinecone? What kind of message?'' Only half paying attention to the whirling green cone, she sprinkled cinnamon and brown sugar on the bowls of oatmeal she'd prepared.

Gracie halted in the arch of the door so fast, the hem of her purple skirt flipped up, down, finally settling around her orange leggings. Jilly winced, but didn't say anything. A woman had to find her own sense of style, even if the woman was only five. Rubbing her eyes, she glanced at Hank. "Why would I put a pinecone in your bed, for Pete's sake?''

"Don't know, sugar. It was there, under my pillow. It didn't blow in through the window.'' He tossed the cone to Gracie. "What do you think, sweetheart?''

Gracie stuck her hands behind her back, and the pine-cone fell to the floor, rattling to a stop in front of her feet. "Nothing." Skirting the cone, she climbed onto a chair. Her orange legs wrapped themselves around the chair rungs. "Yummy. Make a sugar face on top of the oatmeal, Mommy."

As she dribbled brown sugar into a smiley face, Jilly noticed that Gracie wouldn't look at Hank even when he dropped the Gracie-size pair of cowboy boots beside her chair.

"Say thank you, snickerdoodle."

"Thanks." It was a mumble of oatmeal and voice.

"You're welcome, Miss Gracie," Hank replied. "See you later. Or do you want to come with me?"

"I—" Gracie's expression was a mixture of conflicting emotions that Jilly couldn't quite read.

Gracie was up to something, though. "I need to have Gracie with me, but we both appreciate the offer," she said. "Perhaps another time."

Jilly saw the quick exchange of glances between Hank and Gracie, the flash of Hank's grin.

As soon as the door slammed behind Hank, Gracie looked up from her oatmeal, put her spoon down and wriggled her orange feet into the dusty brown boots with their diamond design on the outside. Twisting and turning, Gracie tried to see the entire effect until finally she scrambled to a standing position on the chair and checked herself out in the reflection of the black glass door of the microwave.

Smiling with satisfaction, she lifted first one foot, then the other. "I'm as beeyootiful as Baxter, I do believe. Aren't I?"

Jilly stood next to her, studying the effect of cowboy boots and dress. Gracie never believed a fast answer. "Oh, I think so." She smiled back at the reflection of the smiling child in neon orange leggings and purple dress. "Certainly as colorful."

Gracie patted her dress, twitched her fanny around to the microwave door for a rear view. "Yes, I am very colorful. Nickels would like my boots. Now me and him both have some."

"He and I, Gracie." Jilly hoped some future English teacher would appreciate her efforts. "He and I."

"Could Nickels come again and see my boots?" Gracie wound a lock of Jilly's hair around her short index finger. "Because he didn't see how good a cowboy I am."

"We'll try, doodlebug. I can't promise today, though." Jilly knew Gracie's clock operated on now and this afternoon. Tomorrow was an idea she didn't choose to deal with.

"Please?" The chubby hand stroked her cheek.

"No, Gracie."

"When?"

"When I can. When Nickels—Nicholas's mom lets him. But I promise you that he'll see your cowboy boots."

"I don't like that answer." The soft patting continued as Gracie regarded her pensively.

"I know you don't, sweetheart, but that's the answer."

Touching her dot of a nose to Jilly's, Gracie tipped her head, studying her. "That's the last answer?"

"Yes."

"Okay. But I want to see Nickels *soon*." She hopped down from the chair. "I'll go swing now." She headed for the door.

"Not yet. I have several phone calls I have to make, and then I'll go with you. We'll swing together. In the meantime, while I'm on the phone, will you stir these together out on the porch by the kitchen window and see what happens?" She handed Gracie the plastic bag of flour, the plastic cup of water and the five vials of food coloring that she'd set out on the counter while cooking the oatmeal.

She hoped she remembered correctly that food coloring was supposed to wash out.

"What will happen?"

"I'm not sure. Why don't you see?"

Gracie jiggled the bag of flour up and down as she walked to the door. "P'rhaps it will get hot like Baxter's pink powder?"

"I don't think so. But something will happen."

While Jilly punched in the long-distance number of her lawyer, she heard Gracie murmuring to herself as she mixed flour and water into paste and added food coloring. Chances were, Gracie and the porch would need to be hosed down after the experiment was finished.

When Carl Shaara finally came onto the line, he was guarded, and Jilly's pulse sped up. She knew Carl, liked him. Trusted him. And she could hear in his carefully chosen words that he was trying to be circumspect when what she wanted was answers, explanations, not this professional smoothness. She understood now what Hank had meant about politeness being a cover-up for reality. "Carl," she eventually said in annoyance, cutting him off in midflow, "what's going *on?* Why can't I have access to the accounts?"

Through the window, she saw Gracie thump her fist into the clay ball she'd squooshed together. In her ear, Carl's clipped words about complications made no sense.

"Good grief, if they hadn't offered to make my volunteer job at the hospital a paying position, I wouldn't have any money coming in. But they won't start paying me until I go to work next week, full-time. Carl," she repeated as she walked to the table and rubbed her fingernail under the dots of oatmeal, "what's going on? I know Larry left us provided for. He told me that, over and over, Carl," she insisted, scrubbing at the oatmeal as hard as she was trying to force information from him. "There's the insurance money, the money markets, the funds. All those accounts. Somewhere there has to be some ready money for bills. For day-to-day *living,* Carl," she finished, squashing the desperation rearing its head as she scraped off the last of the oatmeal.

There was no comfort in Carl's distant voice as he repeated something about problems with the insurance. He almost sounded like a stranger. Nothing he said made any sense to her.

"Right now, I don't have enough money to pay a security deposit and first month's rent on an apartment here. And until you straighten out what's going on with the Naples house, I don't have anyplace to *live*, Carl! I can't imagine how the bank could have foreclosed on the mortgage. Larry was careful about things like—" She gripped the pan of leftover oatmeal so tightly that her fingers hurt. "What do you mean, can I wait? I've told you I can't! The next stop is living out of my car!"

Again his distant voice tried to soothe her, and she remembered the reality of Hank's touch on her neck, the comfort he'd given her so effortlessly. In contrast, Carl's attempts were making her crazy with anxiety.

She turned her back to the kitchen window and lowered her voice. "Carl, we have a problem here. Talking over the phone isn't satisfactory. I'm coming in to see you. Have the accounts ready, please. We'll go over them together. None of this makes any sense to me. I'll see you tomorrow or the day after. As soon as I can make arrangements. And, Carl," she said in an even voice, "I can tell you're keeping something from me. Don't, hear?"

Gently, carefully, she placed the receiver back into its hook on the wall.

Facing Baxter had been nothing compared to the cold terror holding her in its grip.

Baxter had been her own fears and memories.

Whatever was going on now affected Gracie, too.

Something was terribly, terribly wrong.

Like crabs scuttling under beach sand, her thoughts whipped out of sight, vanished, and she couldn't think, couldn't plan.

Shaking with coldness, she bent double over the sink, clinging to it.

Chapter Nine

The next two days dragged by on the wings of slugs.

Jilly knew slugs didn't have wings, but in her frame of mind it seemed a fitting symbol for the slow ticktock of seconds and minutes.

Anxiety ate away at her. She called the hospital to see if she could start her job early, but the occupational therapist in charge of interest-level activities for the bone marrow unit wasn't leaving until the following Saturday. She called Carl again, but he wasn't in the office.

She hoped he was in the midst of a stack of papers, burrowing through them until he found a satisfactory answer for her.

Thoughts flickered in her brain like summer lightning off in the distance. A flash: Carl had taken his passport and her money and disappeared. A distant crackle: There never had been any money and Larry was in a witness protection program and—

She tried to ignore the thoughts zapping and zinging through her brain, especially when she caught Hank's puzzled glance as she offered him a second serving of yellow squash from an empty bowl.

"Sorry," she muttered, placing the bowl very carefully on the dining table.

"It's a good way to diet, sugar," he said easily. "Imaginary squash. Make-believe chocolate pudding. Zero calories. You may be on to something here."

She stood up. "I'll get more squash."

Giggling, Gracie lifted the bowl and pretended to scoop from it. "I have delicious macaroni, Mr. Hank. Do you want some?"

"Please." To Gracie's delight, he plopped big spoonfuls of air onto his plate and proceeded to mime the act of eating macaroni.

Jilly couldn't sleep at night and after the first few hours of tossing and turning, she dragged the quilt off her bed and headed for the screened porch. She wrapped the blanket around herself and stared at the starless night while her thoughts circled endlessly.

Larry had had the business mind. He'd been the entrepreneur, arranging deals, moving money from one stock account to another, constantly seeking out the biggest bang for his buck, as he'd told her. Surely Carl hadn't embezzled from all those accounts?

He couldn't have.

Larry would have known. Wouldn't he?

Wind moved through the branches of the oak tree in front of her, and shadows danced across the dark lawn.

Shadows and illusions.

Had Carl played double shuffle in the months following Larry's death? What did she know about Carl, after all?

She wadded the quilt into her mouth to keep from screaming. She knew enough about Carl and Carl's wife, Rainey, that she'd asked them to be Gracie's godparents, that's what she knew. For heaven's sake, she'd trusted him enough to place her *child* into their keeping.

Trusting him with her money ran a poor second to entrusting Gracie to him. And *poor,* of course, was the operative word.

Her tight laugh startled a creature poking around in the bushes. Unless Carl could find his way through the paper trail, she was going to be literally down to her last dollar.

So much for her plan to leave the ranch.

Without money, she had no place to go for the moment. She couldn't ask her friends to let her bunk with them, not now, not with this cloud hanging over her. There would be no way of explaining what had happened.

Pride kept her from making any calls.

She'd already been in the position of poor relative once in her life. If it weren't for Gracie, she'd sooner sleep in her car than ask her friends—

But they weren't her friends.

Frowning, she sat up straighter in the chaise longue.

Rain pattered on the roof, bringing with it the rich smells of wet earth and the distant corral.

Reality.

The Naples house smelled of French potpourri and air-conditioning. The windows were seldom opened. Larry hadn't wanted the salt-laden air to damage their furnishings.

They'd entertained several times a week in that closed-up house. Entertained friends. Larry's friends. Couples he'd sought out for business purposes.

Where were *her* friends?

Dismayed, she rested her head on her doubled-up knees as she realized what she'd let happen in her life.

She didn't have any friends apart from Larry, and he was gone. Over the years, she'd drifted away from all the friends she'd had in high school and college. The only people she could truly call friends now were the people she worked with at the hospital.

And Callie.

Hank? Hank Tyler wasn't a *friend*. She couldn't ask him for the kind of help she needed.

Not after that kiss.

There was no one she could, or would, ask for help.

Before anyone woke up, she went back to her bedroom and changed. She used a concealer stick on the smudges under her eyes and pretended all day that everything was peachy keen.

On his way out the next morning to check on the cattle at the farthest point of the ranch, Hank brought her a jagged stone, fist-sized. "Another gift, Jilly?"

"What?"

He laid it on the table beside a platter of pancakes.

"Did it wake you up, Mr. Hank? Is that what happened?" Propping her chin on one hand, Gracie regarded him thoughtfully. "You woke up 'cause the stone was poking you in your behind or your very tender toes, didn't you?"

Hank tapped the stone thoughtfully as he regarded her for a long moment. "No, Miss Gracie, it didn't wake me up. It rolled out from under the foot of the bed when I was digging around under the covers for—" He cast Jilly a harassed look.

She rescued him. Gracie didn't need to know he was probably fishing around for his briefs. Or whatever. Heat flamed in Jilly's face as she met his gaze and thought of those missing shorts. Or whatever.

"For his socks, Gracie."

"Oh." Gracie frowned. "It's a pretty big rock, Mr. Hank. *I* would have known it was in *my* bed," she scolded. "It would have woked me up for sure."

Even in her sleep-deprived fog, Jilly recognized that her daughter's interest in the rock seemed a trifle excessive. She couldn't find the thread, though, that would lead her into the cave of her daughter's thinking, so she shrugged and murmured, "Sorry Hank," and returned the milk carton to the refrigerator, wondering why she'd taken it out in the first place. She was saying sorry too much. She needed to ground her thoughts so that her mind could function without this overload of panic.

On her own, without Gracie, Jilly knew she could manage financially. But Gracie— Oh, God, Gracie needed shots and new shoes and— Thoughts zipped and sizzled in her brain.

Gracie needed so much.

The second night it rained again. The edges of the porch were dotted with rain, but Jilly pushed the chaise longue up against the house wall and huddled in a waking sleep as the silver rain curtained her view. Drifting in and out of hazy dreams, she ran down dark, rainy streets desperately seeking something she'd lost. In one dream, she was running up and down the streets of Chicago—and she'd never even been there—looking for Gracie and Cletis but seeing only the tip of the traveling cat's tail, hearing only the faint giggle of her daughter.

Hank found her on the porch before she could slip back into the house.

"What's the matter, Jilly?" Shirtless, he was in his unsnapped jeans, his hair rumpled and sleep-bent. The watery morning sunshine gilded the lines of his chest muscles, gilding them until he seemed like a golden-brown marble statue as he stood there motionless, watching her. And then he rolled his shoulders and yawned, his jaw popping with the effort. "Bed not comfortable?"

"The bed's fine." She thought she glimpsed the edge of white elastic riding above the top of his waistband. "I thought fresh air would be nice. I got up early."

"Liar, liar, pants on fire," he said as his mouth stretched in another cracking yawn. "You've been here since before midnight. I heard you come out last night, too, sugar." Sleepy-eyed, he strolled toward her. "And you've been on the phone every day."

"I'll write Callie and T.J. a check." She drew her knees up to her chin.

"Oh, swell, I'm sure glad you planned on doing that, sugar. I'd hate to think you were going to skip out and leave them holding the bill for calls to exotic places like—Aruba. And the Bahamas." He leaned against the railing. "Make sure you don't round it off, either. You know, cheat them of a dime or two." Underneath the tigerish sleepiness, his gaze was shrewd, fixed on her. "What's going on, Jilly?"

In the distance, a blue jay scolded.

"Nothing."

He stooped beside her, resting a fist on either side of her, anchoring the quilt to the chaise. He rubbed his forehead against hers, and as his beard-rough chin scraped hers, all she could think of was that he was a man in love with a shadow.

"Don't give me that look, Jilly."

She knew which look he meant, and she couldn't help the compassion welling up inside her for this man who'd sacrificed his life for his brother's happiness. "All right. I won't. How about this one?" She crossed her eyes and stuck out her tongue.

"Much better." He touched the tip of her tongue, and her toes curled. "Now, do you want to tell me why you're camping out on the porch?"

The heat from his chest was warmer than any the quilt had provided. She folded her hands into a fist and kept them safely under the quilt.

But even with anxiety coiling inside her, she wanted to see if the gleaming skin of his shoulders and chest was as warm, as smooth as it looked.

He bumped her chin with his. "Come on, sugar. It won't kill you to share a little of the load."

Leaning her head against the back of the chaise, she shut her eyes. "Gracie and I are going to Naples tomorrow. To see my lawyer. Some business matters. There's a problem with Larry's estate. With the will. I'm not sure."

"I see."

His tone of voice made her open her eyes. His expression carried more understanding than Jilly had, and she was suddenly glad he didn't ask any more questions. Looking at his closed-off face, she felt very fragile and very, very scared. She didn't want to know what he was thinking. "Everything's fine. Just a minor matter of paperwork." She closed her eyes again, frightened by what she saw deep in his eyes.

"I'll fly you down this afternoon in the Cessna." His voice was rough, a slide of anger in the low tones. "I have a beater car at the airport outside there. Unless you mind riding in a banged-up, rusted-out beater?" The mockery was there but tinged with challenge.

She opened her eyes. The challenge was for her, the anger wasn't. "Very good, Hatty."

He tapped her chin gently with his index knuckle. "Cheap shot, princess."

"You're clever. If I say no thanks to the plane offer, I look like a snippy ingrate who thinks she's too good to ride in—what did you call it?—a banged-up beater?" She let her head fall back again and watched a spider flit across the horizontal board above the screen door.

Like the fly the spider was after, she was caught in a sticky web. She wanted to take Hank up on his offer. It would be faster than the long drive. And she knew him, knew the way he could exasperate her into laughing with his teasing, knew the way he made her skin heat and tingle with a glance. Around Hank Tyler, she wouldn't have a spare second to make herself crazier with apprehension.

"It's a *very* banged-up beater," he said gravely, imitating Gracie. "And I would be *very* insulted if you didn't take me up on my offer, Jilly."

"Why are you offering, Hank?"

"Because of these." He smoothed his thumb over the circles under her eyes. "Looks like you took a piece of charcoal and got ready early for Halloween, sugar."

"You have to quit flattering me like this. You'll turn my head. A woman can only stand so much sweet talk, you know."

"We could take a quick swing down to Okeechobee and let Gracie stay overnight with Nickels." Like Jilly, he'd slipped and used Gracie's nickname for Nicholas. "That would give you as much time as you needed. And Gracie, well, we *know* how Gracie would like the trip, don't we?"

She didn't fight the upward tug at the corners of her mouth. Even now, he could make her smile. "Ah, you are a tempting devil, aren't you?" Jilly sighed. "To use my daughter against me." Gracie would be beside herself with excitement. "What about Sarah? She might not be ready for company. And Nicholas might have school."

"That can all be checked out, sugar. I don't know about Jake, but Sarah loves company. Give her a call." He stood up, wide awake now and preparing for action. "We could be there in an hour."

"You have other things to do. The ranch. The horses."

"Nothing that can't wait."

His offer felt like charity, and she resisted it. But, finally, he made it impossible for her to refuse.

"Please, let me do this for you, Gillian." A flush stained his sharp cheekbones. There was no laughter in his square face, no teasing in his sea-green eyes.

"Why?"

"Because everybody needs a shoulder to lean on once in a while. Because I think you need a friend right now. Let me be that friend."

Jilly's eyes prickled with tears. She nodded, unable to speak. "All right. I'll call Sarah."

She went into the house and made the call. Karma. Serendipity. Some things were just meant to be. Nicholas's school had two days of teacher conferences. Sarah would be thrilled to have Gracie visit.

"What about Jake?" Jilly twisted the phone cord. She didn't want to intrude on the two of them. Hank had told her they'd been married only eight months.

"Jake? Poo," Sarah said with a laugh. "He'll love having Gracie here. He's nuts about kids. We'll take care of your Gracie, Jilly."

"I know." Jilly twisted the cord again. Hank had told her about Sarah and Jake. About Jake's child. Sarah's. "I know."

By the time Gracie got up, Hank had returned to the house to see if the arrangements were locked in. When Jilly told him everything was set, he went to his room to pack his gear. Finished, he stuck his hand out for the cup of coffee Jilly offered and sat down at the table next to Gracie.

Puffing at a strand of hair, she was slouched over a bowl of cereal and bananas. She looked up quickly and back down at the lake of flakes and yellow slices as Hank placed a twelve-cup muffin tin on the kitchen table.

"Notes are nice, too," he said with a questioning lift of one eyebrow and a fast glance at both Jilly and Gracie.

"Hmm." Jilly decided that she needed to have a talk with her daughter. Gracie was obviously the culprit, but why she was putting objects in Hank's bed was beyond Jilly.

"You waked up?" Gracie said hopefully, puffing away at her bangs.

"Nope. Slept like a hound dog after a hunt." Hank lifted a strand of Gracie's bangs. "I see. It is Miss Gracie under there. I wasn't sure for a second."

"It's me." She slumped in the chair. "Just me under here."

Hank let her bangs settle in place before saying casually, "Want to go see Nickels and spend the night, Just Me?"

Gracie bounced. She shrieked. Her bowl of cereal tipped, rocked and milk splashed onto the table. Hank handed her a paper towel and she wiped it up with a swoop and a swipe across the table, chattering away the whole time.

Jilly blinked and found the three of them in Hank's plane. Gracie didn't get airsick. The trip went like butter on hot toast the entire way. They dropped Gracie off with Sarah and Nicholas, and Gracie trotted off without a backward glance. The beater car was, in fact, a very respectable four-door hatchback in excellent condition.

And then, before she could take a deep breath, they were at Carl's office. Jilly didn't like the way she kept sticking dollar signs on landscaping, artwork, office furniture, but she couldn't stop tallying prices. Her head was reeling with approximate sums.

It was clear that Carl was doing extremely well.

She tripped at the edge of the burgundy and green carpet in the entrance to Carl's suite. Hank's cupped palm steadied her, kept her from banging her hip against the burled walnut bookcase inside the door he opened for her.

Darla, Carl's receptionist, smiled and waved her on through to Carl's holy of holies. Jilly pasted a matching smile on dry lips and gave Darla a small wave.

There had been pity in Darla's smile.

This was going to be a very bad hour.

Hank gripped Jilly's elbow and turned her to him. "I'm going to meet a friend. Beep me when you're ready." He handed her a slip of paper with his number.

"Fine. Thank you." The paper fluttered between her fingers and she tucked it out of sight into her purse, snapping the catch.

Her face was pale, set with determination, and her arm trembled under his fingers. A fine tension vibrated through her, carried to him. She shouldn't have to face what was ahead of her in that office alone, but she would.

He couldn't help her. She wouldn't welcome his company in there, wouldn't want to know he was seated in this high-powered reception area waiting for her, so he'd lied and made up an errand.

Every instinct he used in flying told him that it was going to be rough for the princess. Whatever Carl Shaara had told her had been the tip of the iceberg, but it was bad enough. Hank had seen the deep smudges under her eyes, the white lines around her mouth.

He wanted to throw her over his shoulder and ride the hell out of Dodge, take her to safety somewhere where there weren't lawyers with accounts and bad news. The misty blues and greens of her suit and silky blouse made her seem like a sea nymph caught in ocean spray, fragile, ephemeral. He wanted to capture that moment, freeze it. Not let her go into that office and hear what she was going to hear.

With his own two hands, he wanted to kill Larry Elliott. It was a good thing the man was dead.

But there wasn't one damned thing he could do except drop his hand, lean down and press a kiss onto her startled mouth.

She started to speak, but he didn't let her. "Hang tough, sugar," he muttered and stomped out the door.

Larry Elliott had been a fool at best.

Downstairs a woman went from columned ashtray to ashtray, smoothing the sand and imprinting it with the logo of the building. No sooner had someone used it than the woman raked it clean and restamped it.

Hank went outside. Thinking of Jilly upstairs with Lawyer Shaara, he found the building too claustrophobic. He checked his watch and left the business area proper, heading for a fast walk down Vanderbilt Beach Road, passing the hotels that virtually glittered with five-star ratings.

This was where Jilly had lived with her husband. Where she'd bought her sleek Italian shoes. Where she'd raised her indomitable Gracie. It would be easy for a girl to become a princess in this town where the very air he breathed seemed to taste of dollars and diamonds.

He missed the smells of the ranch. He missed the feel of a horse under him, the slide of a rope through his gloved hands.

He passed a garden café advertising grilled pompano and grouper, Florida stone crabs. In its window, he saw himself striding by in jeans and leather jacket, mouth grimly tight, eyes narrowed.

He missed ranching, the rhythm of its days. It was a way of life he found himself craving as he walked the beautiful streets and passed the lavish stores. In the distance, the ten-mile stretch of palm-lined sugar-white beach sparkled like the glass of the store windows.

This was where the princess belonged. But he didn't.

In fact, once he'd left the ranch, he belonged nowhere. For fourteen years, he'd been as rootless as a tumbleweed, blowing hither and yon, never settling.

Coming back for T.J.'s wedding had thrown him for a loop.

When he'd kissed Jilly, that sense of homecoming had uncovered buried memories, awakened forgotten dreams. There had been that moment when he'd felt as if the earth had shifted beneath his feet, changing everything, and now he couldn't seem to get a handle on what he wanted.

He knew what he *didn't* want anymore. He didn't want to be one of the vast, anonymous herd, moving from place to place, leaving nothing of value behind them after they were gone.

And suddenly, wandering the sun-rich, money-gilded streets of this manicured town, he discovered that he wanted to go home again, really go *home*.

He wanted a place he could call his own.

Like his father, he wanted to leave something behind him, a legacy of courage and hope and faith in the goodness of life.

Running both hands through his hair, he laughed out loud, a sharp bark that made a woman in a designer suit turn and stare. Head averted, she sped up, her heels clicking rapidly away from him down the sidewalk. Amused by her, amused by his folly, he laughed again.

Hell of a thing for a man to discover that what he'd given away was the very thing he needed.

He slowed as he walked back toward the law offices. He'd sold his share of the ranch to T.J., but there were other possibilities. Some things could never be the way they were. But life could change.

Back in the entrance to the building, he waited patiently for Jilly as the minute hand on the discreetly placed clock inched forward.

It was worse than he'd thought.

Shell-shocked, her face tight and pinched, she was another person from the Jilly he'd grown accustomed to. He almost didn't recognize the woman who walked into the lobby. She was Jilly, but not *Jilly*. He went right up to her and put his arm around her waist.

"Okay, sugar?"

"No. But I will be." The coldness in her voice frightened him. She'd been cool, reserved, but never cold, never this glacial woman with a face taken from a Greek tragedy. "Will you take me to the house? The one that was—mine?"

"Of course." The steely strength that he'd learned she possessed was all that was holding her upright. "How about a cup of hot tea first?"

"Tea?" She looked right through him, as though he wasn't there, and needing to make contact with the woman he knew, he took her chin in his fingers, held her head still. "Tea?" she said. "Now?"

"Jilly, what happened in there?"

Her laugh rose unsteadily, but it was so controlled that he frowned. "Nothing. Everything. Please get me out of here. *Please*." Her voice sent shivers over him.

"All right. Do you have tea or coffee at the house?"

"I haven't the slightest idea." She walked rapidly ahead of him, and if he hadn't been faster, he reckoned she'd have walked right into the glass doors of the lobby exit. "But I want to see the house one more time. And there's a picture of Gracie I want. That's all I know."

* * *

It was a house fit for a princess, all right, he mused as they drove up the long driveway. A beachfront home along Gordon Drive, it looked as if it had been picked up from the Mediterranean and put down in Florida. He might have mistaken the huge place for a hotel if Jilly hadn't been giving him directions. From the back, the house would have a view of the Gulf of Mexico and the blinding white beach that stretched along the coast.

Hank didn't even want to think what a place like this had cost. He hoped that whatever had happened, Jilly would be able to salvage financial security from the sale of the house. If she could, she'd be set for years.

There was a Realtor's lockbox on the door, and she dialed a combination and opened the door.

The entrance was marble and glass, red brocade benches, Waterford chandeliers. It was a foyer designed to impress anyone walking into the house, designed, Hank decided as he turned slowly around and looked at the area, to intimidate. It was not a welcoming entrance to a home.

"No," Jilly said as he turned around and whistled, "I didn't decorate it. Larry hired someone. I've forgotten whom." She pressed her fingers to her eyes. "I have to go upstairs. The picture is there."

She walked off, leaving him standing at the foot of the curving, wide staircase that rose majestically to the second floor with its enormous, windowed landing.

With all the glass and windows, the damned house would cost a fortune just to cool in the summer. A chill moved down his spine as he watched Jilly walk up the carpeted stairs and disappear.

He couldn't see her living in this house. Hell, he couldn't see how Gracie had survived five minutes in this place. There wasn't a fingerprint on a pane of glass, there were no toys. There was nothing that indicated that a small girl had lived in the house for five years.

That Gracie, with her energy and curiosity, with her wide-eyed delight in life, had lived here disturbed him. It was hard enough to imagine Jilly, but *Gracie,* that bundle of charm and guile...

Hank felt sick as he looked around him once more, seeing the glossy finish of the doors, the dustless finish of the tables in the hall. It was a house of silences and glass, of threat and overwhelming power.

He knew now as much about Larry Elliott as he ever wanted to know, and he despised the man. The intensity of his hatred shook him, made him clasp the newel at the bottom of the stairs with a grip that almost ripped the wood off its post.

It was the tinkle of breaking glass that sent him racing up the stairs, flinging open one door after another until he found Jilly.

An aroma of perfume overwhelmed him as he stepped into the room and saw the sparkles and shards of glass sprinkling the lavender carpet. Jilly's shoes didn't even dent the thick pile of the carpet of what was apparently her bedroom.

Hers and *Larry's.*

The mirror in front of her was shattered, and even as he started to ask her what she was doing, she reached down and picked up a perfume bottle, flinging it at the mirror with such cold fierceness that Hank fell silent.

She was all calm elegance on the surface even as she grasped another bottle and sent it sailing in a perfect arc at the mirror.

And then her eyes met his in the reflection, and he saw the baffled fury behind her control. "I don't understand. I don't understand why Larry did this...."

It was said so softly that it took Hank a second to process what he'd heard. "Did what, Jilly?" he asked carefully, walking slowly to her as she took a vase off a shelf next to the long bureau with the shattered mirror. "What did Larry do? What's happened? What did Shaara tell you?"

The vase smashed against the mirror and fell silently onto the carpet.

Hank had a feeling there had been a lot of silences in this room, a lot of things left unsaid.

Tears slipped down her pale cheeks as he reached out for her. "Don't touch me." Her hands were palm up, stopping him. A tiny trickle of blood ran down her hand. "Don't!"

"Aw, sweetheart," he said, and gathered her close to him. He meant only to comfort her, to calm her agony even though he didn't understand it.

But she was shaking to pieces in his arms and he wrapped himself around her, thigh to thigh, hip to hip, the softness of her breasts flattening against his chest as he absorbed her tremors.

"I can't stand it!" Her fists drummed against his shoulders, and her forehead thumped his chest once. "Oh, God, I can't breathe! There's no air in here!" Her head twisted back and forth, and she plucked at the neck of her blouse.

He cupped her head with one hand and unbuttoned the top three buttons of her silk blouse. "There, Jilly, take a deep breath. Easy, sweetheart. You're going to be all right. I'm here."

The fierceness of her emotions hummed between them, buzzed in him as her body shook against his.

And comfort changed to something else as she stood on tiptoe and curled her arm around his neck. Her fingers were ice against the heat of his skin. "Hank, please. I'm lost in here. I'm numb in here. Make me feel *something!*"

He lifted her right off the floor, swinging her around until they were no longer facing the mirror that reflected shattered lives, shattered expectations, and he set her on the edge of the bureau and kissed the skin at the base of her throat.

His anger, hers, their emotions merged, melted together as he bent over her, his mouth tracing the vein that ran along the side of her throat, following it to her jawline and then, with a sudden inhalation, he took her mouth with his.

There was no comfort in his kiss.

There was hunger and need and loneliness. His.

There was confusion and anger and need. Hers.

Her head fell back and she whimpered, pulling his head closer to hers as her mouth opened. He couldn't get close enough, couldn't find the angle he needed, and he nudged her knees apart, sweeping her right into him with one hand around her fanny. And still she wasn't as close as he wanted her to be, as he needed her to be.

Cradling her against him, he lifted her off the bureau and to him, clipping her ankles around his waist. Her suit skirt slipped above her knees and he urged it farther, stroking the sleek nyloned length of her legs.

Her shoes fell silently to the carpet, landed in the glass sparkling around them.

Her tears were wet against him as she buried her face in his neck. Her breath was warm on his damp skin and he shivered, gathering her to him and stumbling drunkenly, blindly, to the bed, needing to feel all of her against him, needing to touch her, needing to ease the aching inside him.

She was underneath him, the slick surface of the bedspread cool to his hands flattened on either side of her head. Her hair fanned across the lavender and gray spread, and he lifted one strand, wound it around his finger and kissed her again, not thinking of anything except the wonder filling him, the warmth of her skin.

She kissed him as if he were the only thing in her world, gave him his kisses back with tenderness and hunger, lifting to his touch, touching him with her cool, slim hand, heating his skin with the ice of her own.

And then she stopped. Abruptly. As if a switch had been turned off inside her. He heard her whimper.

"No. I can't. I don't want this. What are we doing?"

He rose from the bed and stepped back, away from her. He knew what they were doing. What they *would* have been doing in three more minutes if she hadn't stopped, but he couldn't speak. His blood was pounding thickly through his veins, an aching pleasure that wouldn't be satisfied.

But it was her choice.

She rolled to one side, drew her knees to her chest. The hem of her blue skirt lay like a brand across her smooth thigh. "Larry borrowed against his life insurance. Mortgaged the house. There's nothing left except debts. Huge debts. More than I could repay if I lived to be a hundred." Her voice was dead, drained of life. "None of this—" she waved her hand vaguely "—is paid for. Everything was bought on credit, paid for with loans that have been piling up interest."

"Do you hate him?" Hank shook with fury at the man who'd left her and Gracie so defenseless.

She sat up clumsily, her skirt hitching up as she scooted to the edge of the bed. Her face was bleak. "Of course I don't. How could I? He did it all for me. For Gracie. He wanted us to have the best. What kind of person would I be to *hate* him after all he did for us? I don't hate him."

"How forgiving of you, princess." He couldn't stand her defense of a man he understood too clearly.

Her head lifted slowly and her eyes looked lost. "He did it for me, you see."

"No, princess, I really don't see at all." Hank wanted to shake her out of her lethargy. The minute he'd walked into the house, he'd understood her husband, and he couldn't believe that she was still trying to find excuses for him.

"He tried to give us what he thought we wanted. He worked himself to death. That's why he had the heart attack, Carl said."

Fury at her insistence in preserving an illusion roared through him. How could she keep defending Elliott? No wonder she kept her emotions on a short leash. Hank couldn't ever remember feeling the kind of anger that snapped inside him and made him careless. She had to see what she was doing to herself, to her life. To her daughter.

He paced in front of her. "Did you ask Larry for all this stuff?" He had trouble even saying the name.

"No." She shook her head wearily and her damp cheeks caught the last of the sunlight shining through the windows. "He thought I needed it."

"Did you?"

"Of course not. I hated it. Oh, God, I *never* wanted this." Passion rippled across her face. "But Larry did his best. I have to remember that, at least. Everything he did, he did for us."

"Why, princess? Why do you need to forgive him, to turn him into some kind of saint? Do you like living in the past? With an illusion? Is that what's going to keep you warm at night in the years to come? An illusion?"

"What are you doing?" she wailed. "Why are you saying these things to me?"

He lifted her by her arms until she was standing toe to toe with him. "Because you needed me to make you *feel*, Jilly. And because I want to know if you prefer the illusion of a saint to a living, breathing man, princess, that's why. I want to know if you like living in your ivory tower. I want to know if you're always going to stay hiding behind your nice, polite mask, princess."

"Mask? You think *I'm* hiding behind a mask?"

The whiteness of her strained face almost destroyed him, but he couldn't stop. Anger and something else were pushing him forward.

"I'm only a man, princess, and maybe a man isn't what you want in your life. Maybe you'd rather sleep with memories. Is that how it is for you, Gillian? Is that what you want? To live your life behind walls and masks?"

Chapter Ten

"That's rich." Stung, Jilly pulled away from him, her face burning. "You're a fine one to talk about living in the past, Hank Tyler. How *dare* you attack my memories, my marriage, when you've spent your entire adult life living in the past."

"Better spell out exactly what you mean, sugar," he drawled, and she heard the male anger.

"All right." She stooped and picked up her heels, slipped them on, needing their height. "You're the one who hides behind a mask. You smile and joke and laugh, and no one ever sees the real you in back of all that teasing."

"And what is the real me?" He stalked her to the door. "This is what you almost said earlier, isn't it? So what am I hiding, sugar, since you think you know?"

"That you've been in love with Callie Jo for years."

He went still, the anger draining from his face. "In love with Callie?"

Tiredly, Jilly plodded on. He'd pushed her too far. She hadn't wanted to tell him this, but he'd tramped all over her own memories. "You know what I mean. Everyone believes you're lighthearted, easygoing, but you've been running away for years. Running away from your real feelings about Callie. You've never made any commitments to anyone or anything over the years. Tell me, please, exactly *who* is living in the past?" She'd done it, crossed a line, and there was no going back for either of them. "I'm right, aren't I?"

"Yes." He turned on his heel and left the room.

Picking up the picture of Gracie in the silver frame, Jilly left, leaving the door open behind her. Someone else could clean up the glass. The house wasn't hers, never had been. None of the furnishings, not even the thick towels and soaps. None of it was hers or Gracie's.

Everything would be sold. She could declare bankruptcy, but she intended to pay off what she could, sell her car, sell her jewelry, her furs. Everything. Then she and Gracie could start over.

But in the meantime, she had nowhere to go.

Waiting in the driveway, Hank held open the car door. "Get in, Jilly. You're coming back with me to the ranch, but we'll stay here overnight and pick up Gracie tomorrow." He clipped the words out.

"I can't." Humiliation washed over her. She couldn't afford a motel room. There were things she had to do. She didn't mind doing without, but she hated having to depend on someone's charity.

"What are you going to do then?" He leaned against the car and waited.

There was, of course, nothing else she could do. Her job was at the hospital in Tarpon City. She couldn't strand herself here. She had no way of getting to Gracie. "Thank you," she said stiffly.

"You're welcome," he mocked.

Hank found a motel not far from the airport and checked them into separate rooms. "You can pay me back later."

That was the last thing either of them said for the rest of the evening. He picked up a bag of carry-out hamburgers and drinks, knocked on the motel-room door and handed one bag to her. She shut the door behind him and collapsed onto the bed.

Jilly pulled back the covers and lay down in her slip. Trucks and cars roared past all night long. She wouldn't have slept, anyway, not with Hank's words chasing her own thoughts.

She had kissed him, had asked him to kiss her. Everything that happened afterward had been her responsibility. She'd needed something, *someone,* to break through the ice surrounding her.

He had.

But then, from the first moment she'd met him, Hank Tyler had broken through her barriers and made her feel all kinds of emotions.

And now she would have to deal with the consequences of her actions.

Splashing water on her face the following morning, she thought over her options. She would stay at the ranch until her job started. Hank had offered, and she would find some way to repay him eventually. She could take out a loan from the hospital credit union and find an apartment.

And then she would sign all the papers Carl sent her.

They picked up Gracie, who wept as they drove away from the Donnellys' house and fell asleep on the flight back to the ranch. Hank tied the tarp over the plane and drove them all back to the ranch. He teased Gracie, asked Jilly questions and no one would have known he was in pain.

But Jilly did. She'd hurt him, and there was nothing she could do to take back what she'd said. She joined him in the game of let's-pretend that they played for Gracie, for each other so that they wouldn't have to face what had been said.

The next morning, Gracie crawled into Jilly's lap as they were sitting at the kitchen table. Hank had left the house before sunup. Jilly had heard the clunk of his boots on the porch, heard the slam of the door and had stayed under the safety of the quilt.

"Mommy." Gracie stuck her thumb in her mouth.

"Yes. Gracie?"

"I thought he was a prince."

"What?" Jilly smoothed Gracie's hair back and hummed. "Who? Nicholas?"

"No. Mr. Hank. I thought he was a prince. But he never woked up like the princess in the story. She knew there was even a teeny-tiny pea under *her* mattress. But Mr. Hank *never* knowed there was anything in his bed." She rubbed her face against Jilly's breast. "I love Mr. Hank 'cause he taught me to ride and be a cowboy, and I wanted him to be a prince for you."

"I don't understand, doodlebug. What are you talking about?"

"Mr. Hank." Gracie sighed. "Daddy always said you and me were his princesses in his kingdom, and I wanted to find a prince for you."

"Why?" Jilly thought about Larry and his princesses and his "kingdom." She thought once more about princesses and the waste of their lives.

"Because you are lonely. So I tested Mr. Hank to see if he is a prince, with the rocks and pinecone and muffin pan. But he is not," Gracie concluded sadly. "He is only a man. Not a prince at all."

"No, sweetie, he's not a prince. He's just a man."

Jilly looked up from Gracie's bent head and saw Hank's long, denimed legs halted on the porch outside the kitchen window. He'd heard everything.

Her heart ached for him.

Later that day, she called the hospital credit union and made arrangements to apply for a short-term loan. Then she and Gracie went apartment hunting. Even though she had nothing, not even furniture, there was a strange pleasure in finding an apartment that suited them both. The landlord of a small garage apartment agreed to wait.

She was on the phone talking with Carl about selling her jewelry, when Hank returned for dinner. He tipped his head and studied her for a long moment before heading down the hall for a shower. He didn't say anything, though.

And, after all, Jilly thought, what was there to say? What had to be done, had to be done. For thousands of years women had coped with much worse than what she was going through.

She wished, though, that she could get past the sense of betrayal that Larry's behavior left her with. Betrayal. She knew she shouldn't feel that way. He hadn't betrayed her. He'd made bad decisions, bad judgments.

Guilt became a constant companion through the next days. She couldn't forgive herself. Couldn't forgive herself for not loving Larry the way she should have, couldn't forgive herself for not somehow making it clear to him that she hadn't needed any of the *things* with which he'd filled their lives.

At dinner every night, Jilly lit candles on the dining room table of the ranch house and tried to avoid the appraising looks Hank sent her way.

As each day passed, Jilly felt as if she were waiting for the eye of the hurricane to pass.

And then Carl called again. They talked for a long time, and the last of the scales dropped from Jilly's eyes. Hank was right. She had created an illusion. For Gracie? For herself because of the guilt she'd only recently recognized? If Hank hadn't yanked her out of her rut, she would have turned Larry into someone who'd never existed in real life.

Halloween evening was cool, crisp, dry. Hank insisted on taking her and Gracie into Tarpon City for trick-or-treating.

He needed candy, he told Gracie, and he'd be real hurt if they didn't let him come along.

Gracie wore her ruffled purple dress, cowboy boots and a battered cowboy hat Hank found for her. "I'm a cowboy princess," she said, bouncing into Hank's car.

"Really? I should have known, but I didn't see a crown. I'm sorry, Miss Gracie."

"Cowboys have *much* more fun than mootant morfers, and princesses get to wear beeyootiful dresses." She twisted and turned in the front seat. "See how beeyootiful I am, Mr. Hank?"

Hank laughed. "You're the most beautiful cowboy princess I've ever seen, sweetheart."

It was the first time Jilly had heard him laugh since their trip to Naples.

"Oh, thank you." Gracie kissed his cheek. "You're beeyootiful, too."

And in that instant when Hank tucked Gracie under his arm and fastened her seat belt, Jilly knew she loved him.

As they walked down the tree-lined sidewalks of the small town, Gracie rushed ahead of them, ringing doorbells and dipping into low curtsies as people dropped candy into the paper bag she'd decorated herself with pumpkins and scraggly stick-figure cats drawn in lurid shades of pink and yellow.

"Jilly—"

"Hank—"

They stopped under a palm tree as Gracie ran to ring the doorbell of Hank's former grade-school teacher. A goblin raced behind her and they were joined by a small ghost in pink sneakers.

"Hank, perhaps you were right. I think in some ways I have been trying to excuse so much of what Larry did." She laid her hand on his arm.

"Wait, Jilly." His muscles tensed under her hand. "Let me go first."

"No, Hank, I need to say this although I don't know how to explain it." She sighed as she watched Gracie and the pink-sneakered ghost swap candy. "At some level, I've always known my marriage was a sham, but it was so important to me to make it work. I didn't love Larry, though." Her voice shook. "You have no idea how hard that is for me to say. For years, I've said I loved him, automatically. I wanted to. I tried to. But I didn't. I wanted a home, a family. And I never understood until recently that Larry wanted *things*. Everything was for show, for impressing people. And Gracie and I were part of the set decoration. We were nothing more than possessions to him."

"I shouldn't have said anything." He covered her hand with his. "I should have kept my mouth shut."

"No, you were right. In more ways than you know." She shrugged. "Carl told me today Larry even had funds set up for... his girlfriend. He was paying for an apartment in Miami for her. Country-club membership. Everything." She rubbed her neck. "I lived for years with guilt because I thought it was my fault that he worked so hard, that he gave us all those things I didn't want and Gracie didn't need. It was never for me and Gracie. Everything he did, he did for himself. So that he could impress people. That's all." She heard the bitterness and regretted it, but it would take time for her to get past the betrayal—she'd been right about that, after all—and past the bitterness. "Did you know that at first the police thought loan sharks had killed him? Or that he'd killed himself in desperation over gambling debts? If it weren't for the waste of it all, it would almost be funny, wouldn't it?"

"No. It's not funny." Hank brushed the side of her neck, and she shivered at his touch. "Jilly, I'm no prince, and Lord knows you deserve one, but I love you."

She stared at him. "You love Callie. You have for years. I know that. You even admitted it."

He nodded uncomfortably. "But I was a boy when I fell in love with her. I'm a man now and I want a home. A *life*. You were right. But I think you and I could build a life together. We could make each other happy. We could give Gracie a good home. I'm crazy about her." He paused and looked at her intently. "Could you live with a cowboy? Could you see yourself living on a Florida ranch with no frills?" He stumbled over the words, and Jilly thought he'd never been so awkward in his life. There wasn't an ounce of smoothness in his words or in his uneasy stance as he rocked back and forth on his heels, his hands jammed into his back pockets. "I couldn't give you everything, but I'm not poor, either. I have money saved. Hell, I haven't spent money on anything for years except my car and the plane. Can you see that kind of life, Jilly? For Gracie? For you?" His voice dropped and he scuffed the sidewalk with the toe of his boot. "Think about it."

She wished, oh, she wished he wasn't in thrall to a ghost from his past, wished for things that could never be.

"It won't work, Hank," she said gently, finally. "I won't live my life playing second fiddle to something or someone else ever again. I want to share my life, I'm willing to work as hard as I know how to make a good marriage, but I won't create another illusion. You're still in love with Callie. I can't marry you." She hooked her finger in his shirt pocket and pulled him close. "But I wish I could. If I thought a marriage between us had half a chance, Hatty, I'd race you for the marriage license."

"It would work." He slid his arms around her. "Take a gamble, Jilly. On me. On us. I swear, I'd make it work."

"I know you would try." She swallowed. "But there would always be that ghost between us, Hank. And Callie's my friend. T.J.'s your brother. Can't you see how impossible it would be? The built-up emotions would blow up sooner or later." She wiped her eyes against his shirt. "You're the one who said people needed to be up front about their feelings. Needed to argue and yell a little. Can't you see how the silences would build up?''

"Yes." He stroked her back. "But it doesn't have to be like that, sweetheart.''

"I've had the silences, Hank. I want something real this time. Something all my own. Not second best. Even with you." She swallowed her sob and gave him her best smile. "And damn your devil-eyes, I'm in love with you, Hank Aaron Tyler."

"Well, shoot, sugar." He kissed her, his lips and body singing a siren song of seduction and persuasion.

And she kissed him back, kissed him with the love filling her heart and flooding her soul. She knew now what a real marriage could be and she let her body and her touch speak for her, let her kiss tell him everything.

Halloween was over, but the ghosts lingered.

Gracie moped, missing Nicholas. Jilly sold her car and sent Carl the difference between its price and that of the used car she bought. Every bit helped, and it seemed necessary to her to ease her conscience of as many of Larry's debts as she could, even though she told herself they were his, not hers. As she dropped the cashier's check in the mail, she wondered if she was being foolish.

The next day, having slept on the decision, she understood that her actions had to do with karma, with New Year's celebrations, with clean slates. With psychic handwashing.

Hank teased her, cornered her in the hall, left rocks and pinecones on her bed.

She laughed, she splashed water at him when he crowded her at the sink, she played tag football with him and Gracie and they both fell on her in a combined tackling effort.

And with Hank's laughing eyes looking into hers, she went weak inside. It was so *easy*, so *right*.

But Gracie, her chaperon, her Jiminy Cricket, was always there.

Every time Jilly saw Hank, she had to bite her lip to keep from whimpering that she took it all back, they *could* work it out. But she didn't.

That strength came from a place inside her she'd never known. And she was grateful to Hank for giving her the key to the door.

Without him prodding and pushing at her, she would have remained a sleeping princess, when what she wanted was to be a partner.

Callie Jo and T.J. returned early two days later. Watching Hank hug Callie, Jilly wanted to weep once more for the way fate played its hand of cards sometimes. If she'd never been married to Larry, if she'd never seen how pretense could destroy people, she might have taken Hank's gamble without a second thought.

Over the top of Callie's piled-up hair, Hank stared into Jilly's face. Her dusky blue eyes were sad, but her expression was serene, at peace.

Pride.

Lord, the woman had pride. And grit and strength.

He looked down at Callie. "Welcome home, sis." He grinned at her, his heart beating slowly and evenly, his pulse thumping along at its normal rate, and the world shifted again, one final time, and everything was clear to him at last. "Missed you guys. A little, anyway." He slapped T.J.'s shoulder and turned Callie loose.

"Didn't miss you, Hatty. Not a bit." T.J. gave him a squeeze around the shoulders. "Ranch looks good."

"I know," Hank said smugly and tried to keep Jilly within view.

It should have been easy. The princess had abandoned her earth-toned clothes for a screaming neon tangerine skirt and top. It should have looked awful. But the top kept sliding to one side and then the other, revealing the delicate round caps of her shoulders. She looked altogether delectable, and he had an irresistible craving to nibble at the shoulders peeking in and out of that sherbet-colored top.

But every time he tried to talk to Jilly alone, she had Callie with her. Or Gracie. Or T.J. was hanging around like a burr under a saddle. Hank had about decided he was going to have to lasso her and drag her off behind the horse corral if he wanted to talk to her.

And he did. He had things to tell her elegant self. Things she needed to hear.

By evening, Jilly had vanished, taking Gracie with her.

Even with Callie and T.J. and Charlie home, the ranch seemed empty.

Hank missed Gracie's eyelash-batting. He missed her rocks and tests. He missed the diminutive feminine presence more than he'd ever dreamed he could.

As for Her Highness, well, there was no telling what he'd do once he had his hands on her again. And he intended to have his hands on her—soon. On her neck, her tush, her mouth. Oh, he had plans for her, he did.

But she wouldn't see him when he went to her apartment. She hung up on him when he called.

Finally, in exasperation, he tracked her down at the hospital. He couldn't go into the bone marrow unit without a mask and paper booties over his shoes, so he outfitted himself, scrubbed his hands with antibacterial soap and stomped off in search of her. He saw her through the blinds of a boy's room.

She was showing him how to work the exercise bicycle in the room. Listless, the boy ignored her. His face was swollen and shadowed, and a rolling IV pole was next to his bed.

Hank listened to the low murmur of Jilly's voice, heard the boy finally chuckle in answer to something she'd said, and then, damned if the woman didn't start singing her Cletis song.

When she left the room with a wave and a husky encouragement to the boy to keep exercising if he wanted to get his counts up high enough to go home, Hank grabbed her and waltzed her past the double doors and into the general hospital area, backing her into the linen closet.

"Okay, Jilly, why can't I see you? Why can't I see Gracie?" He cornered her between a rack of thermal blankets and a stack of pillows.

"Because," she wailed and buried her face in his chest, gripping his shirt with her narrow hands.

"There's an answer for you." He lifted her tearstained face. Her eyes were as beautiful as ever. He hadn't forgotten that deep, dusty blue that made his heart turn over. "Stupid mutt that I am, though, damned if it makes any sense to me." He kissed the tear trembling on one eyelash. "Mmm. Nice." He dipped his head. "Think I'll take seconds." He did. And thirds before she shoved him away. "Explain *because* to me, sugar."

"Because I don't have the strength to resist you, that's why. And I won't let myself in for the grief of loving you, Hank Tyler, not when you're all mixed up inside about loving Callie, loving me. I couldn't stand it."

"No?" He kissed the tip of her reddened nose. "You're sure?"

"Completely."

"All right." He lifted his arms and freed her. "Come to Thanksgiving dinner, Jilly. Four o' clock. You and Gracie, okay? Do that, at least. Tell Gracie to wear that spiffy orange and purple outfit. I'm wild for that look." He backed out of the closet, leaving her dabbing at her eyes with the corner of a blanket. "I'm counting on you. Callie wants you there. Be there, Jilly, or I'll come after you. And, Jilly—"

"Yes," she said in a tear-clogged voice. "What?"

"I bought a ranch."

He left her chewing on that piece of information.

* * *

Until three-thirty, Jilly wasn't sure she was going to go to the Tylers' Thanksgiving. It would be uncomfortable. Painful. She would be miserable watching Hank casting sheep's eyes at Callie. No, she wouldn't go.

Hank had sent Gracie an invitation of her own. It had a photo of Nicholas on it, and Hank had sketched in a Gracie-figure and an enormous wildly colored turkey. Gracie held it up to Jilly. "I have to go, Mommy. It says R.S.V.P."

It did. They went.

And Jilly sat among the crowd of relatives and friends. She ate lumpy mashed potatoes and something Nicholas called Auntie Bea's puke-purple Jell-O. The potatoes were delicious. The "puke-purple" Jell-O was swell if she shut her eyes.

And throughout the dinner, Jilly watched Hank with his sister-in-law. He helped her carry in the platter with the turkey on it while T.J. cuddled Charlie and gave him a bottle. Jilly watched Hank take a towel and flick it at Callie's charcoal-gray lined slacks, tagging her on the fanny.

And slowly, Jilly began to smile.

Something had changed.

Hank was treating Callie like one of the boys.

After the dishes were done and half the crowd was settled in the living room in front of the TV for the football game, Hank snagged her elbow and marched her outside.

The fresh air woke her up out of the drowsy state she'd slipped into. "Come with me to the swing, Jilly, will you?"

"Perhaps," she teased. "Why?"

"Because I have something I want to show you." Taking her arm underneath his, he tucked her hand against his rib cage.

Jilly liked that, liked being able to feel his lungs expand, contract, with each breath. It felt very—companionable.

Under the oak tree, Hank lifted her onto the swing. Her skirt puffed out and she kicked off her shoes, letting them fall to the ground as she stood up on the swing and faced Hank who came up to her chest.

He lifted an eyebrow. "Nice view, sugar." Mischief sparkled in his green-blue eyes as he handed her a wadded-up gray lump. It was the shredded remnants of the cardboard crown she'd been wearing that first day, the crown Gracie had stuck on her head. "Gillian, sweetheart, you can be a princess if you want to, a mutant morfer—whatever the hell that is—or a cowboy princess. You can be whatever you want to be, sugar, whatever you want to become."

Jilly draped her arms over his shoulders as he pulled himself up on the swing beside her. The swing wobbled, shuddered, held as Hank bent his knees and pumped the swing slowly back and forth. Jilly decided she liked this, too, and she held him around the waist as he pumped the swing higher. Her skirt wrapped around his legs, between them. The cardboard crown was a tiny lump in the pocket of her skirt.

"That's a lovely speech, Hatty," she said teasingly into his ear as the swing glided back and forth past the trunk of the tree. "What's the point?"

"The point is, sugar—" he slid one leg between hers and adjusted the pendulum balance of the swing "—the point *is* that I'm asking you to share your *self* with me. That's all I want. You. Whoever you are. Whatever you decide to be. I want you with me, Jilly, by my side. I don't want to go through the rest of my life alone. And, no matter what, sugar, without you, I'll be alone." His voice dropped and he bent his knees a bit more as he blew against the bottom of her earlobe. "I'm not a saint, I'm not a myth and I'm damned sure not a prince. I'm just a cowboy, Jilly, a man who loves you. Don't let me turn into a crotchety, lonely old cowboy, Jilly. Let me into your life. Into Gracie's."

"You love me, don't you?" She was suddenly seized with shyness and delight.

"Oh, hell, yes, princess. Why did it take you so long to figure that out?"

And then her cowboy kissed her for real, right there on the swing where anybody looking out the front room could see them. Jilly heard Gracie and Nicholas laughing, she heard T.J. shout something and then she didn't hear anything else except Hank's heart beating against her, his voice murmuring the silliest things into her ear as he propelled the swing high into the bright blue sky.

*   *   *   *   *

HE'S NOT JUST A MAN,
HE'S ONE OF OUR

Fabulous Fathers

FATHER BY MARRIAGE
Suzanne Carey

Investigator Jake McKenzie knew there was more to widowed mom
Holly Yarborough than met the eye. And he was right—she and
her little girl were *hiding* on her ranch. Jake had a job to do, but
how could he be Mr. Scrooge when this family was all he wanted
for Christmas?

Fall in love with our Fabulous Fathers!

Coming in December, only from

Silhouette
R O M A N C E™

MILLION DOLLAR SWEEPSTAKES (III)

No purchase necessary. To enter, follow the directions published. Method of entry may vary. For eligibility, entries must be received no later than March 31, 1996. No liability is assumed for printing errors, lost, late or misdirected entries. Odds of winning are determined by the number of eligible entries distributed and received. Prizewinners will be determined no later than June 30, 1996.

Sweepstakes open to residents of the U.S. (except Puerto Rico), Canada, Europe and Taiwan who are 18 years of age or older. All applicable laws and regulations apply. Sweepstakes offer void wherever prohibited by law. Values of all prizes are in U.S. currency. This sweepstakes is presented by Torstar Corp., its subsidiaries and affiliates, in conjunction with book, merchandise and/or product offerings. For a copy of the Official Rules send a self-addressed, stamped envelope (WA residents need not affix return postage) to: MILLION DOLLAR SWEEPSTAKES (III) Rules, P.O. Box 4573, Blair, NE 68009, USA.

EXTRA BONUS PRIZE DRAWING

No purchase necessary. The Extra Bonus Prize will be awarded in a random drawing to be conducted no later than 5/30/96 from among all entries received. To qualify, entries must be received by 3/31/96 and comply with published directions. Drawing open to residents of the U.S. (except Puerto Rico), Canada, Europe and Taiwan who are 18 years of age or older. All applicable laws and regulations apply; offer void wherever prohibited by law. Odds of winning are dependent upon number of eligibile entries received. Prize is valued in U.S. currency. The offer is presented by Torstar Corp., its subsidiaries and affiliates in conjunction with book, merchandise and/or product offering. For a copy of the Official Rules governing this sweepstakes, send a self-addressed, stamped envelope (WA residents need not affix return postage) to: Extra Bonus Prize Drawing Rules, P.O. Box 4590, Blair, NE 68009, USA.

SWP-S1195

HAPPY HOLIDAYS!

Silhouette Romance celebrates the holidays with
six heartwarming stories of the greatest gift of all—
love that lasts a lifetime!

#1120 *Father by Marriage*
by Suzanne Carey

#1121 *The Merry Matchmakers*
by Helen R. Myers

#1122 *It Must Have Been the Mistletoe*
by Moyra Tarling

#1123 *Jingle Bell Bride*
by Kate Thomas

#1124 *Cody's Christmas Wish*
by Sally Carleen

#1125 *The Cowboy and the Christmas Tree*
by DeAnna Talcott

COMING IN DECEMBER FROM

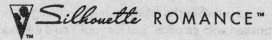

Silhouette

SPECIAL EDITION

TM

®

CELEBRATION
1000

It's our 1000th Special Edition and we're celebrating!

Join us these coming months for some wonderful stories in a special celebration of our 1000th book with some of your favorite authors!

Diana Palmer
Debbie Macomber
Phyllis Halldorson

Nora Roberts
Christine Flynn
Lisa Jackson

Plus miniseries by:

Lindsay McKenna, Marie Ferrarella, Sherryl Woods and Gina Ferris Wilkins.

And many more books by special writers!

And as a special bonus, all Silhouette Special Edition titles published during Celebration 1000! will have **<u>double</u>** Pages & Privileges proofs of purchase!

Silhouette Special Edition...heartwarming stories packed with emotion, just for you! You'll fall in love with our next 1000 special stories!

1000BK-R

Silhouette ROMANCE™

COMING NEXT MONTH

#1120 FATHER BY MARRIAGE—Suzanne Carey
Fabulous Fathers
Holly Yarborough was just another assignment, but that didn't stop Jake McKenzie from falling for the sexy female rancher. When Holly learned the truth, would Jake lose his new bride?

#1121 THE MERRY MATCHMAKERS—Helen R. Myers
Read Archer's children wanted a new mother and Marina Davidov was perfect. Little did they know that years ago, she had broken his heart—could Read give their love a second chance?

#1122 IT MUST HAVE BEEN THE MISTLETOE—
Moyra Tarling
In a long-ago night of passion, Mitch Tennyson had transformed Abby Roberts's world. Now Mitch was back, and Abby felt forgotten love mixing with the fear that he could learn the true identity of her son....

#1123 JINGLE BELL BRIDE—Kate Thomas
Matt Walker needed a wife—fast. And sassy waitress Annie Patterson seemed to fit the bill. With his cowboy charm he won her hand. Could she find a way to lasso his heart?

#1124 CODY'S CHRISTMAS WISH—Sally Carleen
All Cody wanted for Christmas was a daddy—and a baby brother! Would Ben Sloan be the right man for his mommy, Arianna? Only Santa knew for sure!

#1125 THE COWBOY AND THE CHRISTMAS TREE—
DeAnna Talcott
Crystal Weston had an ideal marriage—until tragedy tore it apart. Now her husband, Slade, had returned to town, determined to win her back. But would the handsome cowboy still want to renew their vows once he met the son he'd never known?

You're About to Become a
Privileged
Woman

Reap the rewards of fabulous free gifts and benefits with proofs-of-purchase from Silhouette and Harlequin books

Pages & Privileges™

It's our way of thanking you for buying our books at your favorite retail stores.

Pages & Privileges ™

✂

┌─────────────────────────────┐
│ **PROOF OF**   SR-PP70   │
│ **PURCHASE**   │
│ Offer expires October 31,1996 │
└─────────────────────────────┘

**Harlequin and Silhouette—
the most privileged readers in the world!**

For more information about Harlequin and Silhouette's PAGES & PRIVILEGES program call the Pages & Privileges Benefits Desk: 1-503-794-2499

Silhouette®
™